Kate has three notebooks, the Red,
Yellow and Blue Notebooks, in which she
records her life. Through reading,
writing, living and learning to love,
she discovers things about herself
that she never expected.

Praise for Joanne Horniman's previous novel,
A Charm of Powerful Trouble

'A tight, intriguing, beautiful story' www.theblurb.com
'Not to be missed' *Magpies*

SECRET
SCRIBBLED
NOTEBOOKS

JOANNE HORNIMAN

ALLEN&UNWIN

For APW and LGN

First published in 2004

Allen & Unwin
83 Alexander Street
Crows Nest NSW 2065
Australia
Phone: (61 2) 8425 0100
Fax: (61 2) 9906 2218
Email: info@allenandunwin.com
Web: www.allenandunwin.com

National Library of Australia
Cataloguing-in-Publication entry:

    Horniman, Joanne.
    Secret scribbled notebooks.

    ISBN 1 74114 406 X.

    I. Title.

    A823.3

Cover and text design by Sandra Nobes
Typeset by Midland Typesetters, Maryborough, Victoria
Printed by McPherson's Printing Group

10 9 8 7 6 5 4 3 2 1

secret scribbled notebooks

The Red Notebook

Hello, Red Notebook! Of the three notebooks I bought, Red, Yellow and Blue, you are the one I most want to write in. What is so special about the colour red? Is it that it's the colour of blood – of life; of Lil's favourite lipstick?

You smell (I have just sniffed you) clean and sharp and a bit spicy. Some books smell of mushrooms, but by the time you have developed that mushroomy odour I will be an old woman.

For posterity (I love that word), for the people who might unearth you from a forgotten attic or trunk, I will offer the following information:

My name is Kate O'Farrell and I am seventeen years old. I live in the town (some like to call it a city, but a real city must be more exciting than this place is!) of Lismore, on the north coast of New South Wales. I am in my last year of school, and when that is over I will be leaving this place for good – going to a proper city, where I will begin my new life.

I have long red hair and pale skin. I like staying up very late at night. It is my ambition to see the sun rise, but sadly I am always asleep by then. I love eating and reading, preferably at the same time.

I am very tall, and too thin.

I have never been in love.

I don't know what I want to do with my life, except that I want it to be exciting, and full of people and places. Maybe I'm just another wannabe girl writer, but I won't admit to it.

I would really like to be a tree. Not for ever, just for a little while. A mango perhaps, with lots of sheltering leaves and luscious fruits.

But for now, I live in a house called Samarkand with my sister Sophie and an old woman called Lil, who will not say how old she is. Sophie tells me that Oscar Wilde said to never trust a woman who reveals her age – she'll reveal anything. Since I have already revealed my age to you, perhaps I will end by revealing anything (and everything). I don't know yet. Can I trust you? Notebooks have been known to spill secrets.

I have never been touched by death or disaster.

I should say, though, that my sister and I are virtually orphans. Only virtually, because our parents didn't die, they simply disappeared. And not even in mysterious circumstances. They left us when I was three.

I have, however, just recently been touched by life! Less than twenty-four hours ago I became an aunt! My sister has had a baby – a girl, called Anastasia.

I love her!

(Oh. My accompanying music is Crowded House, 'It's only natural'.)

Sophie started reading to her baby in the fifth month of her pregnancy, so by the time she was born, my adorable baby niece was wonderfully well-read. She was familiar with Oscar Wilde, James Joyce, W.B. Yeats – Sophie had a thing about anything Irish – and *Anna Karenina*, of course, which although it wasn't Irish was Sophie's all-time favourite book.

The Baby (because that was what we called the foetus) was very appreciative. She kicked and danced about, and Sophie's otherwise perfect oval of a belly was always being pushed out of shape by a foot, an elbow, or possibly a head or a backside, as the baby rearranged her position. (We were always sure she would be a girl. We were also certain that she would have a lively and original character.)

Sophie was often too weary to read. She'd moan, 'Read to us, Kate.' I could never get my head around James Joyce, so I read to Sophie and her unborn baby the poems of Yeats. One in particular, 'The Song of Wandering Aengus',

3 notebooks   3 secret scribbled notebooks

I read time and again. I especially love the last verse for its rhythm, and its longing.

> *Though I am old with wandering*
> *Through hollow lands and hilly lands,*
> *I will find out where she has gone,*
> *And kiss her lips and take her hands;*
> *And walk among long dappled grass,*
> *And pluck till time and times are done*
> *The silver apples of the moon,*
> *The golden apples of the sun.*

Sophie's baby was born in early spring, not long before I finished school. A message was brought to the classroom when Sophie went into labour, and I tore off to the hospital on my bicycle straight away. I was one of two official birth helpers, so they allowed me into the labour room, but when I got there all I could do was stand and gawp.

Lil was the other helper. She was feeding Sophie bits of ice, and when the pain got really bad, she cried to the nurses, 'Oh Gawd, can't you give the poor child something for this?'

'No!' cried Sophie. *'No drugs!'*

But she was in such pain. I couldn't bear to see her like that; I thought she might split open, like an egg. Earlier on she had been reading *The Collected Works of Oscar Wilde* between contractions to cheer herself up, and I took hold of the book and held onto it, hard. Later, I noticed that my fingernails had dug little half-moon impressions into the cover.

The Baby certainly took her time to be born. I walked Sophie up and down the hospital corridors for what seemed like hours, stopping whenever she felt a contraction coming on. When she implored me to rub her lower back, I rubbed it, until suddenly that wasn't what she wanted at all, and she snapped at me to stop. Finally, well into the early hours of next morning, the Baby decided it was her time to come into the world, though she wasn't so much born as shot out, red and angry, her limbs flailing with unexpected, terrifying freedom.

It must have been awful for her, to come so quickly from a confined, dark place to brilliant light and endless space. She wailed fit to wake the dead, until she was swaddled tightly by the comforting restraint of cloth. She had been covered with a gleaming, bloody, cheesy substance, which the nurse partially wiped away before wrapping her. Then she was placed at Sophie's breast. Lil stroked the top of the baby's head. 'What a perfect little darlin',' she said.

The baby looked like one of those Russian dolls, a bundle of cloth with a rather stoic little face emerging from it, dominated by bright, dark, knowing eyes. I imagined her clicking open to reveal, magically, a set of identical dolls in descending order of size. She was the beginning of *us*, our first descendant, the only other person we knew on this earth to be properly related to us. I thought that her life should be recorded in words and pictures and perhaps even song.

Sophie named her Anastasia.

It was almost dawn by the time the initial excitement died down. Lil had kissed everyone she could get her hands on, reaching up to grasp the sides of their faces with her old hands and puckering up her creased red mouth far too early for the actual kiss. The doctor looked very surprised to be rewarded by a kiss from Lil. If I hadn't been so over-whelmed and pleased by becoming an aunt, I'd have died of embarrassment.

When there seemed to be nothing else to do, the nurses said that we should allow Sophie to rest. 'Kate, bring me back something new to read!' Sophie cried as I made a lingering exit from the room, reluctant to drag myself away from the baby. 'Bring me something interesting!'

An inkling of light had appeared in the sky. I waited with Lil on the footpath for the taxi. 'Anastasia!' said Lil in a tone of disbelief. 'It's a big name for a baby.'

I stood awkwardly, straddling my bicycle. I can't think of words to express what I was feeling – fear and wonder and awe and exhilaration might be a start. I wanted to get away from Lil to savour my feelings privately. 'I'm going to tell Marjorie,' I said, and pedalled away down the silent laneways that surrounded the hospital, my headlight making a wavering beam in the darkness. When I arrived at Marjorie's place I had to sit beneath a tree for a few moments to gather myself together, though where it was all the parts of me had gone, I couldn't say. I sat there in the near dark, and dew came down on me, and finally, when I felt I could be with people again, I went to Marjorie's window, and threw pebbles at the glass to wake her (I've read of this in books and had always wanted to do it).

Marjorie had been my best friend for a long time; I knew that she would wake at once. She is one of those rare people who open their eyes and jump out of bed looking as fresh as . . . a daisy. I've seen her do this when I stay overnight, and it's a bit scary. I don't know if she ever needs sleep, really, or if she goes into a kind of suspended animation. And her pyjamas are never creased or wrinkled or even worn-looking.

She let me in the back door. Her excitement ('A girl!' she kept saying, as if she couldn't believe it, 'A girl!', though I'd been telling her for months that was what the baby would be) . . . her excitement finally allowed the whole amazing thing to sink into me, and we jumped up and down on the spot for a little while, though this was something neither of us would normally do.

We made hot chocolate. Marjorie was in her mauve chenille dressing-gown, and her knobbly sleeve kept brushing against my arm as she moved about the kitchen. Despite the jumping up and down I was still in a daze, and Marjorie took hold of me and sat me down in a chair. Marjorie's parents came out in their dressing-gowns. 'It's a girl,' I told them. 'We're calling her Anastasia.'

'Ah, the legendary survivor of the Romanovs,' said Marjorie's father, raising both eyebrows and stirring his chocolate with a slow, even movement. He was a doctor, a general surgeon, tall and thin, with humorous, watchful eyes and hairy wrists.

I sat at the table and savoured the warm, full feeling that welled up inside me. It was a feeling that was absolutely new to me, and I sat and talked to Marjorie and her family and basked in it until Marjorie's mother stood up to make toast.

It was then I remembered that Lil would be wanting help with the breakfasts at Samarkand, so I tore myself away and pedalled like a mad thing through the streets that were already crawling with leisurely cars.

Samarkand was still shrouded in mist, and it rose up like an apparition, enormous, ramshackle and old. It sat on a bend in the river, like a monument to earlier times, and had a view up an uninhabited stretch of water fringed by trees. Standing on top of high timber stumps (the underneath was a barren area regularly swept through by floods), it was two-storeyed, weatherboard, with deep verandahs, and a staircase zig-zagging up the front, punctuated by landings. The galvanised iron roof was almost entirely red with rust.

I dumped my bike at the bottom of the steps and bounded up them, two at a time. SAMARKAND, said a name-plate fixed to the wall near the front door, in mirrored letters on oiled wood. If I peered into the worn, silvered surface, I could make out the tops of trees, and the sky, and bits of my own face – an eye, a scrap of red hair, a freckled forehead.

I used to pause and gaze from the verandah, across the square grassed area directly in front, not quite a park, with a line of palm trees down one side. In front of that was a road, then the river. My secret childhood cubby was down there – an enormous fig tree which looked almost human, but which I also imagined was a rambling, spacious house, full of long corridors and secluded rooms.

But I didn't have the luxury of daydreaming now, with breakfasts to be served. Lil was in the kitchen, cracking eggs into a bowl with one hand and throwing the shells onto a plate, where they landed with a brittle sound. She had bandy legs and hunched shoulders; she seemed to be shrinking inside her skin each day. The sun streamed in through the windows onto the worn green walls. The coloured panels at the top of each window – gold, purple, green – threw jewelled squares of light into the room. It was an ugly room, but this morning it looked beautiful.

I made piles of toast (I love toast, and think one should eat as much of it as possible), took it out to the dining room and went back to fetch the scrambled eggs. At the largest table that morning was a young man with a mournful face and long matted hair and bare feet, and a woman who kept crumbling her toast into bits and pushed away her plate of eggs without appetite. They were not together, but it appeared to me that they matched. At a small table next to them, a shabby businessman bent anxiously over a sheaf of papers, sipping coffee.

'I'm sorry, we're a bit at sixes and sevens this morning,' said Lil, bustling into the room, 'but Sophie had her baby in the early hours. Imagine! A girl! Anastasia, her name is. She's beautiful – I'm over the moon, I can tell you!' She beamed at all the guests in turn and twirled around and danced back into the kitchen.

The guests had no idea who Sophie was, but Lil's joy infected them, and they smiled shyly at each other with wary eyes. Their bodies softened and relaxed; they swayed gently like tentacled creatures in a rockpool stirred by a passing current. The thin woman pulled her plate towards her and began to eat, after all. The mournful young man leaned across and asked the businessman whether he minded if he looked at his newspaper.

I could see through to the kitchen where Lil was dancing to music from the radio. She moved easily and gracefully, her arms above her head and her feet making intricate patterns on the floor like a Greek dancer. Lil often danced alone this way. She sashayed into the dining room and threw her tea-towel and apron onto the back of a chair. 'I'm done in,' she said. 'Let's leave the dishes in the sink for once; I'm going to get some sleep.'

I hoed into my breakfast, my head full of the baby. This *girl*, whom Sophie had named *Anastasia*. Neither of these words seemed to do her justice. I remembered her private little face as she lay sleeping against Sophie's breast. She seemed to me to be not so much a child as a flower bud, or a newly-emerged butterfly, damp, enfolded, and full of promise.

The Red Notebook

Music: Rickie Lee Jones, 'Chuck E's in love'

    Found at Hope Springs:
    A Room Of One's Own, by Virginia Woolf, $3
    The Journals of Anaïs Nin, Volume Five, $4
    also, a boy (beautiful), brown and slender, whose name
I don't yet know

So far, Red, you are the only notebook I have written in.
Yellow and Blue lie languishing, waiting for me to feel the
urge to use them. But what shall I write in them? I feel
your impatience. You want more from me than random
scribble, but will you get it? (Wonder all you like – only
time will tell.)
    I want, I want, I want . . . At this point I'm just a mass of
seething wants, but what I want I'm not really sure of. (Like
going to the fridge and opening it, 'letting all the cold air out'
as Lil complains, and not knowing what it is you want to eat.
You stand with the door open hoping that something will

inspire you.) I'm standing with the door open at the fridge of life, and I want.

Sometimes I think I'd be happy if I could just make sense of all the fragments of my life.

The day Anastasia was born I went out and bought three notebooks with shiny covers and fragrant paper to scribble down my secret thoughts. Three was probably excessive, but I couldn't choose which one I liked best: the red, the blue or the yellow. I love stationery, and can never resist a fragrant piece of paper or a pen with a nice grip that writes in a pleasing way upon the page.

Then I went off to find a book for Sophie. Down an alleyway off one of the shopping streets is a place with the tantalising name of Hope Springs. It's a second-hand bookshop run for charity, and the proceeds go to projects in East Timor and refugee support. I went there sometimes because it had an air of possibility, and I love all places where books are gathered en masse. At Hope Springs the books were like flotsam and jetsam that had been washed up by the tides. All sorts of unexpected little treasures were possible. I imagined that the books would be encrusted with barnacles and salt, spilling sea water when you opened them, but I only ever saw an occasional silverfish and a lot of dark

2 notebooks 13 secret scribbled notebooks

spotting on the pages, like the marks on old people's hands. But against the evidence of all those sad, unwanted books, I went there the afternoon after Anastasia was born because I felt a trickle of hope (hardly a spring) that there might be something there that Sophie would like.

The shop is staffed by volunteers, a changing cast of people who give the general impression of advancing age and wispy beards and unironed clothing. But on this particular day there was a boy there, not much older than me, with a slim, slightly stooped body, olive skin, and a graceful, rather hooked nose. He stood beside me and gave a hint of a smile as he placed a book on the shelves. His fingers were long and brown and slender, and so were his eyes. Every part of him was brown and slender. Someone, somewhere, had constructed him perfectly.

There is nothing like browsing in a bookshop for covertly observing someone. I felt that the boy was observing me too, but we were both also eavesdropping on the conversation between two other customers. They were middle-aged people with shapeless bodies clad in jeans and big shirts, and were lamenting the lack of standards in written English these days: the mis-use (or even non-use) of apostrophes, the bad grammar that cropped up even in Published Books, and the dirty-mindedness and lack of plot in these same Published Books. Finally they walked out of the shop, and the boy and I looked over at each other at the same time.

'I hope you know where to place an apostrophe,' he said, softly.

'I most certainly do. A badly placed apostrophe is something that really turns my stomach.'

'And I hope you always observe the correct English usage.'

'I wouldn't dream of corrupting our fine language. And as for Plot – if I ever write a book, I will make sure it has a good, soundly constructed Plot.'

'I don't know how these Modern Novels get published,' he said, shaking his head, still in the same deadpan voice.

'It's a scandal and a disgrace.'

At that same moment I found a book by a writer called Virginia Woolf. It was called *A Room of One's Own*, and though it looked very dull from the outside, with a stained hard cover with no dustjacket or picture on it, I opened it and liked the way the words were put together. It was about women and fiction and looked just the thing for Sophie. I also found (I'd been looking in the 'Women's Literature' shelves – how ridiculous, bookshops never have a section called 'Men's Literature') a book whose cover photograph attracted me at once. On it, a woman reclined on a bed with her hands behind her head and stared frankly at the camera, her pale face framed by a mass of dark hair. *This is who I am*, she seemed to be saying. She wore a lacy-looking blouse patterned with dark leaves, and had an exquisite china-doll face, with thin eyebrows and a cupid's-bow mouth. *The Journals of Anaïs Nin*, the book was called.

I took the two books to the table that was used as a counter, and the boy came over to serve me. He smiled when he saw what I was buying, but he didn't comment and, despite our earlier banter, I felt suddenly tongue-tied. I paid for the books and left without asking his name or anything, but once I was out on the street I regretted it. I wanted to go back at once, because I couldn't wait to see him again, but I was too shy to turn round.

I gave *A Room of One's Own* to Sophie that afternoon, but could see that it would be a while till she would be strong enough for such a book. All her desire for something *interesting* to read had disappeared; she declared that her fanny was so sore she doubted it would ever recover (the other women in the room looked at each other and tittered), but that she was still blissfully ecstatic. She added almost balefully that the feeling would probably wear off when the hormones that had kicked in just after the birth wore away. She exchanged glances with the other new mothers around her, as if they were in an exclusive club together.

She slipped the book into a drawer, not even glancing at it, and devoured the chocolate I had brought without offering me any.

I went to see Sophie in hospital every day. On one visit she wept bitter tears, and complained that she leaked from almost every orifice; she waddled to the toilet with enormous pads stuffed down her pants; she held nappies to her breasts to staunch the flow of milk that welled from them at inconvenient times. Otherwise, she seemed very happy. She read snatches of Oscar Wilde and snorted with laughter. She undressed Anastasia and inspected her for any flaws or imperfections and found none. I wondered if she also searched for any resemblance to the man who was the father, but if she did she said nothing. Mostly, Sophie just lay beside her baby and gazed at her. 'She's just perfect,' she said.

Naked, Anastasia was all secret folds of skin, and surprising hairiness. Her mouth was fleshy and dimpled, with all the twirls and convolutions of a flower, her fingers a group of blind, plump grubs. I learned that a baby is not simply a larger person in miniature, but a creature with an almost entirely different terrain. Everything was in the right place but shaped so differently that I was awed to think that she would one day resemble a real, flawed person. Anastasia had the disposition of a baby bird, and either rested in a state of flaccid, helpless dreaminess, or reared up urgently, demanding food.

Because I was at the hospital so often, I was there when the nurses taught Sophie to bathe her, and learned how to test the temperature of the water, unwrap her from the layered confusion of her clothing, and wipe her small protesting face with a warm cloth. I learned how to immerse her in tepid water, where she hung suspended peacefully on my arm like a creature returned to its natural surroundings. I learned how to dry every last tender fold of her skin, and wondered if she minded her lack of privacy, but she bore it all with grace. I thought how amazing it was that Anastasia came to be alive at all. All of life seems so chancey, but each birth must be the biggest miracle of all.

The Red Notebook

Music: none. written in absolute silence

The Journals of Anaïs Nin, Volume 5, 1947–1955

On the cover, Anaïs Nin is a fragile, yet strong-looking woman. She looks fearlessly into the camera. She looks at *me*.

She was a writer, and she lived in wonderful places like Paris and New York, and wherever she went she attracted people like writers, artists, composers and film-makers. Which I have never known (and may never know), but some of the things she says make me feel that I know her.

It says she lived between 1903 and 1977. I'm reading her book and I love it and I can't believe she died before I was even born!

In winter, 1948, she wrote that we receive a fatal imprint in childhood, at the time of our greatest plasticity . . . she writes of the fallibilities, the errors, the weaknesses of parents . . . and more besides. I only half understand this . . . I will keep reading.

I wonder if I read enough about the lives of other

women whether I would find out how to live my own. Whether I'd feel surer about what I wanted to do with myself. Everything that has happened to me up to now has been by chance. I feel that I have been waiting my whole life for something to happen. For someone to come along and change me. Or for a grand event, like in an opera – lots of shrill singing and fancy costumes.

But now, I want to *choose* the way I live my life.

The big question is, How?

The Blue Notebook

All right, Blue. Your turn.

Things are said to come out of the blue. It heralds the unexpected. It is the colour of the sky and Anastasia's eyes. Of rosemary flowers, and memory.

You look like a trustworthy colour. I can tell you everything. Can't I?

I remember . . .

I remember nothing.

The Yellow Notebook

Yellow is said to be the colour of cowardice, but to me it is the colour of optimism. Sunshine. Sunflowers. Egg yolks (which become chickens, if they are permitted to).

I have no idea what I will write next. I will just write.

A girl (tall, with smooth blonde hair caught back with a clip) is walking through a tunnel in the city.

Concrete floor, old tiles on the walls. Grimy. People on either side of her, rushing to and from the trains. She walks slowly, in a pair of dark shoes with high heels (tippy shoes, she teeters slightly). She wears a charcoal-coloured suit – a jacket and tailored skirt. I can't see her face, only her back, as she walks purposefully to the trains.

She's a girl who works in an office. A serious girl. At least, a girl with a serious job – an interesting job. She carries a soft leather briefcase bulging with papers (but not bulging too much). Some work she's taking home?

Where is she going? Who is she?

I finished school the very week that Anastasia was born. At least, I finished that part of school that had to do with going to class each day. There was still the endless study and the exams and the Formal to go, but still, the end of classes was a milestone too.

That night, Marjorie and I sat around a campfire in a paddock with the group of people we had hung around with most of the way through high school (Jason, Nat, Zed, Rueben, Camilla, Zara and Ocean – all of these people had been briefly in love with each other at some stage except for Marjorie and me). We passed around bottles of beer and cider and gave each other occasional sentimental hugs. I looked around at all their faces flushed red from the light of the flames and felt a surge of affection, then leaned back and looked at the stars, and felt my life flowing out from this point, spinning further and further away from this time and these people.

When Oscar Wilde went to Oxford University he said that it was the most flower-like time of his life. It was Sophie who'd told me this, of course; she'd read everything on Oscar Wilde that she could lay her hands on.

I wonder what kind of flower Oscar Wilde would have been? A lily, probably, one of those large, white funereal lilies with an odour of damp melancholy about it. Oscar Wilde, when he was young (going by the photos in Sophie's books), was beautiful, with a full, sensuous mouth and dreamy eyes. That must have been when he was at his most flower-like. When he was older his eyes had a droopy, hangdog look to them, and his mouth looked rather dissipated. He had lived his life to the full and probably squandered a lot of it; he died before he was fifty. The scandal of being sent to jail for his love affair with Lord Alfred Douglas was the end of him.

For years I had been waiting for my own flower-like time to begin. I thought that this would probably happen when I finished school and left Lismore and Samarkand for ever. Perhaps then I could throw all caution to the wind (because I *was* cautious) and become what I was to become.

Perhaps being an aunt would make me braver and less cautious. I had seen Anastasia's eyes open; I was the first person she had seen on this earth. Her eyes had been framed by her damp eyelashes, and they were dark with knowledge. I had known at once that my niece would leave nothing in her life to chance – Anastasia had decided to be born at this time and place and had chosen Sophie to be her mother. Everything that she did in her life would be intentional.

I had known from the start that it would be a wondrous thing to watch a child grow from being a small baby. My own growing, and Sophie's, was shrouded in mystery and forgetting. There were thoughts I didn't allow myself to think, and things that my sister and I never talked about. Our parents had left us when we were very young – almost too young for memory.

Our mother had taken off first. I imagined her becoming airborne like a bird, soaring upwards in a tattered red dress that streamed out behind her like feathers. Afterwards, our father drifted, like a lost boat rather than something of the air, towing the two of us behind him. He washed up at Samarkand. And then left again, without us.

He left us there with Lil, who has looked after us ever since. Sophie told me once that she felt like a forgotten parcel waiting for someone to turn up and claim her. But although I could barely remember my father, I always expected him – he would return one day and our real lives would begin from there. Because I felt sure that our father must have had a good reason for going.

The only thing he left behind apart from us and our shabby collection of clothes was a small box with our birth certificates in it, so he must have known he wasn't returning for a while. And there, with all the authority that printed words on paper confer, is the evidence of our existence, which establishes us as legitimate people for the rest of our lives. Kate O'Farrell and Sophie O'Farrell. No second names, as if our parents hadn't the energy for it. On the certificates are the names of our father and mother. Michael O'Farrell: occupation, labourer. Margaret Thomas, no occupation listed. They weren't married.

Lil had never attempted to find them. Presumably because if people didn't want to be found, it was no use going after them. After all, our father must have known very well where he'd left us.

I often wondered about our mother – this Margaret Thomas, whom I don't remember at all. It is such a stern, forbidding, humourless name, and doesn't match the description Sophie gave me of her. She'd said that our mother's hair was as black as night. She said that she was wanton and wild and gypsy-like, though I don't know how Sophie was able to see all this at the age of five or six.

My mother was never real to me at all; I didn't even quite believe in her existence. But I did have a single memory of my father. It was a memory that led me to believe he would come back. For years I scrutinised every man who turned up at Samarkand wanting a bed, thinking that it might be our father come back to claim us.

The Red Notebook

Sophie is bringing Anastasia home today! We have made
all the preparations for their return. In the storeroom Lil
found an old cane bassinette that she says is a family
heirloom (and we aren't even a proper family!). She
painted it lavender (how predictable!). She also painted
a chest of drawers lavender, for Anastasia's clothes. L is
Lil's favourite colour – ages ago she bought a huge tin of
lavender paint for little jobs around the place, and it never
seems to run out. (How I wish it would run out!)

To compensate for all that Lavender (I want my niece
to have colours other than lavender to look at – it might
become burned onto her retina and scar her for life!),
I have hung a constellation of brightly coloured stars above
the bassinette, which bob about in the breeze. And
Marjorie brought a crystal which we hung in the doorway

to the verandah – we hope it will reflect the river and the sky into the room.

Everything is tidy for once. All Sophie's clothes are put away in the cupboards, nice and clean. This won't last long. Soon she will have them out all over the floor again, clean mixed with dirty, and when she wants to put something on she'll sniff it to determine whether it's clean or not. This isn't the way women are supposed to behave, I know, but Sophie and I have never really learned the proper way for women to behave. We are like savages. Or so Lil tells us, when she's annoyed with us.

But here's the taxi!

When Sophie came home from hospital at last, I was astonished to see her appear in the kitchen the very next morning, 'You look like the wreck of the Hesperus!' said Lil.

But to me, Sophie didn't look like a wreck at all; she looked rather grand, like a boat in full sail rather than a wrecked one. Her faded pink chenille dressing-gown was tied round her waist with a green scarf; her hips swelled out beneath the thick fabric; her breasts were enormous. Crinkled black hair stretched behind her like a cape.

She leaned against the doorjamb. 'I got practically *no sleep*,' she whispered in a voice that sounded as if she had spent the last four hundred years singing jazz in a smoke-filled nightclub. 'Anastasia wanted to feed *all night*.'

I left her sitting at the kitchen table with a cup of coffee in front of her and ran up the stairs. Very quietly, I entered Sophie's room, and though I moved carefully so as not to wake Anastasia, I was hoping that she was awake, or would wake soon.

Even asleep, she was a miracle and a joy to behold. As I bent over the cradle Anastasia must have sensed my presence, because she pursed her lips and grimaced, and then was still again.

Sophie had painted her room vermilion. She said her walls were as red as a womb. Her bed was a voluptuous muddle of sheets and doona, and she had already messed up the room that Lil and I had tidied before she came home. Books and magazines lay all over the floor. The wardrobe contained no clothes, because she'd gone through them finding out which ones still fitted and left them lying all over the floor.

I lay down on Sophie's bed, which smelt of perfume and milk and baby, plopping down onto the pillows and hoping that it would wake Anastasia. I luxuriated in the sensation of being an aunt, noticing how the flimsy white curtains at the French doors billowed in the breeze, thinking I'd like to be a painter and capture the billowing.

A shadow appeared on the curtains. It was Lil.

'Kate, do you intend going to school today, or in the near future, or ever?'

Lil was always convinced that I was hell-bent on avoiding school. I reminded her that it was the September holidays, and after that I was off on swot vac until the exams started.

I examined Anastasia's sleeping face and furled hands. Gently, I unrolled the fingers of one hand, but they curled up again immediately. I thought of how I was waiting for my own flower-like time to begin. You couldn't force a flower. When I was a child I used to pick camellia buds and strip the tightly wadded petals away, one by one, but I never ended up with an opened flower.

Sophie's best friends, Carmen and Rafaella, came to pay homage to the baby. They were lush, seductive-looking girls, with full lips, ruffled blouses that displayed their shoulders, trousers that displayed their belly-buttons, and large hoop earrings dangling from their ears. They were *bold girls*, with dope-smoking hippie mothers, whom Lil had been convinced would lead Sophie astray.

Now they came up the steps like a visiting troupe of gypsy dancers, their high heels clattering along the verandah to Sophie's room, and greeted Anastasia with shrieks of adoration. They'd brought gifts: four pairs of red booties that one of their grandmothers had knitted, and a crocheted hat in rainbow colours. They dangled the booties from their fingers and exclaimed at the impossibly small size, then fitted them onto Anastasia's feet. They pulled the hat onto her head and adjusted it until they felt that it looked just right. Anastasia sucked on her fingers and bore all this with stolid patience.

They wanted to help Sophie bathe her, and when she was undressed they rudely exclaimed over her fatness and hairiness. Even I had admitted to myself that Anastasia was fat (and amazingly hairy), but I wouldn't have said so out loud.

Sophie had given in to her insatiable craving for meat pies when she was pregnant, but there were all kinds of things she wouldn't ingest because she said they 'crossed the placenta': aspirin, and alcohol, and cigarette smoke. Did meat pies cross the placenta? Perhaps this was the explanation for Anastasia's fatness.

Her head was covered with black, straight hair – carelessly stylish. It could well be the best hairstyle she'd ever have in her life. And she had hair all over her shoulders and in a line down her back to her buttocks as well. Sophie said defensively that it was perfectly normal for a baby to have a lot of body hair and that it would fall out soon, but I thought Anastasia might be setting out to be the hairiest woman in history. Because I believed Anastasia knew what she was doing. Already, she knew. She had a strong will, and she cared not one jot what Carmen and Rafaella thought of her.

Carmen and Rafaella had been Sophie's friends since early high school. I watched and vowed that my own friendships would not be like that. Sophie would regularly arrive home in tears and lock herself in her room, sobbing that she was *never speaking to Carmen (or Rafaella) ever again.* That night there would be a phone call and they were best friends again, until the next unkindness or betrayal. 'Don't worry about them, love,' Lil would say to her each time, but Sophie did worry. She desperately needed to belong to them.

They were fiercely competitive. Someone would always be on the outer edges of the friendship. Sophie's love for them both (because it was a kind of love, I can see that now) went through extremes of emotion. They all knew the exact thing to say to cut the other to the heart.

But even though Rafaella and Carmen were so important to Sophie, she was always resolutely herself. They didn't much care for reading, and Sophie did. When she was away from them, Sophie's real friends were the characters she met in books.

She didn't obsess about clothes the way her friends did

either. Sophie was absolutely unadorned. She wore her long black hair loose, or pulled back in a severe ponytail. Her clothes were so dowdy that people thought it was deliberate, a style that she was affecting, but the truth was that Sophie simply didn't care.

But apart from her emphatically unattractive clothing, there was something about her – her face, the way she looked at you, her smile, her way of quoting obscure bits of literature everyone thought she'd made up herself – that made people notice her. They looked, and kept looking, because Sophie was carelessly beautiful. She was splendid and overwhelming, like something in nature that could never be replicated – a mountain, or a river, or a thunderstorm.

Sophie lay on the bed and watched her friends play with her baby, smiling in a detached and almost condescending way. Motherhood had made her more dreamy and languid than ever. All she had done since Anastasia was born was lie on the bed and read and breast-feed.

When Carmen and Rafaella left, the sound of their footsteps and laughter retreating down the stairs, Anastasia started to complain. Sophie opened her dressing-gown, put the baby to her breast, and began to read again. She had been interrupted by the arrival of her friends.

Sophie was reading *Anna Karenina* for the umpteenth time. Her face was absorbed behind the twenty-five-year-old copy of the book she'd picked up at a fete. Nicola Pagett, from the *magnificent BBC dramatization*, stared off the cover to the left, her lips slightly parted, her blue eyes forever a study of hope and anguish. This tale of a respectable married woman in Tsarist Russia who gave up everything for love had a seemingly endless fascination for Sophie.

She put down the book for a moment and moved Anastasia to the other breast, where she sucked intently with her eyes closed before dropping off like an engorged tick and lolling back in Sophie's arms in a milk-induced stupor. Gently, I took her and put her down on the bed. Sophie read on without missing a beat. At last I could observe my niece up close. She was so fat that her cheeks looked wider than the top of her head. I loved her to distraction but was very afraid that she might be the ugliest baby I'd ever seen.

Perhaps she was making a statement, and her disregard for appearance was intentional. Why should babies be pretty? Why should women be beautiful? Though if she did intend being outstandingly ugly, it would be quite an achievement for her to succeed at it. She would be going against her genetic inheritance, because Sophie was certainly beautiful, and Anastasia's father, a guitarist called Marcus who had passed through town with his band nine months before, was more gorgeous-looking than any boy should be. Carmen and Rafaella had said it was a mistake to go out with a boy who was prettier than you were (women were always coming up to him in cafes and telling him he had beautiful eyes), but Sophie wouldn't be told. Now she had Anastasia, and Marcus didn't even know of the baby's existence. Sophie claimed that she was happy to bring Anastasia up by herself, but I wondered about that. I suspected that Sophie had not dismissed Marcus from her mind as she claimed she had. It was possible to spend years filled with hope for something that your more rational self would see as a lost cause. Because hadn't I been secretly waiting for years for our father to return?

A hundred years ago someone like Sophie would have been described as a woman with *a past*. Having 'a past' hinted at something unspeakably shocking that nevertheless everyone must have known of and whispered about behind the tinkle of teacups. Anna Karenina became a woman with a past when she left her husband to live with the man she loved, and she was shunned by polite society. But I agreed with Oscar Wilde: having a past made you immediately more interesting.

When Sophie met Marcus she was working in a coffee shop, and he called her over one day to order another coffee. He wasn't one of the regular customers; she learned that he was the lead singer in a band that was touring the area.

'What do you do?' he'd asked her, after he'd put in his order for a soya-milk latte and the soup of the day.

'Do?' she said.

'For a job.'

'I work here,' she said.

'I know that,' he said. 'But what do you do *really*?'

Then Sophie saw what he was getting at. All of the other people who worked in that cafe saw themselves as being really students or painters or actors, and they were just waiting on tables to pay the bills.

Sophie, in her unremarkable dress, down-at-heel shoes and black cardigan that looked as though it had belonged to a middle-aged shop assistant, adjusted her glasses with their thick black frames, and said again, 'I work here.'

He asked her out as he was leaving. It had to be late,

after his gig, and there was nowhere much to go by that time except his motel room, and they ended up there.

Sophie was almost twenty and had had heaps of boyfriends. Marcus was different. She loved him. She told me this. She only knew him for a bit over a week, but in that time they spent every available moment together. She brought him back to Samarkand, and they sat in the kichen one morning and oozed satisfaction. They were a beautiful couple, both with long dark hair; he with olive skin and she with skin like cream. I saw them once in the street together, Marcus catching hold of her arm and Sophie laughing.

But soon he was gone, on to the next place. He didn't offer to stay in touch.

Can you love someone you've only known a week, I asked her. She said yes. Yes, you could.

'You don't have any control over love. It just is. You can love someone for the way that they laugh, or the shape of their face, or simply the smell of them.'

She couldn't look at me as she told me this. But then, turning to face me with tears in her eyes, she said, 'If you ever have a chance for love, you should take it.'

The Yellow Notebook

The girl in the charcoal suit gets onto a train; as it swerves through station after station, she leans against a wall of the carriage, absorbed in a book. Her journey isn't long. Soon she is at her stop, and she gets out and makes her way up the station steps. Everyone rushes, but she takes her time.

She's in an inner suburb, full of exotic shops. She buys two pieces of Turkish delight for dessert, and passes coffee shops where people lean across tables in earnest conversation. She pauses at a fruit shop where she lingeringly selects mangoes and lychees (they remind her of home, which is a long way away), then heads down a street of tall terrace houses with lace balconies. She lets herself in a front door, painted glossy black.

The house has been made into flats, and hers is at the back – an enormous room with a high ceiling and long windows opening onto a wild garden. She puts down her briefcase and changes into a pale blue kimono with birds and butterflies all over it. She uncoils her hair, shaking it free and separating the strands with her fingers.

It is twilight. She opens the window into the garden and looks out into the trees. Then she makes herself a cup of mint tea, and sits on the floor at the window, sipping it. She sees a movement at the end of the garden. The glint of eyes in the near-darkness. There is an animal out there; it comes and waits between the trees, watching. It knows she is there.

The Red Notebook

Lil and Sophie, today:

– I have a tick in my head! says Sophie, indignantly.

Lil says, – Well, come here and I'll pull it out.

– Last time you pulled one, you squeezed it, and all the poison went in!!!! I had a lump for weeks!!! Get your glasses.

– But I can see it quite well!

– No!

– Don't pull away – I nearly had it then!

Me, wanly: – *I'll* do it. (They ignore me.)

– Ow! You're pulling my hair!

– Do you want it out or not?

– Jesus, I hate this place.

– How did you manage to get a tick anyway? You're always lying on the bed.

– They fall from the trees. They blow in from outside. This place is tick-ridden.

– Got it! There it is. Look at the size of it – tiny. All that fuss, madam, for a little tick. You'd think you'd never gone through childbirth!!

(the exclamation mark was made for us!)

Found at Hope Springs: *The Pillow Book of Sei Shonogon*, for $3

but no boy, of any description, just a man with a moth-eaten beard and wearing an old Fair Isle jumper

Music: Sinead O'Connor, 'Factory Girl' and Joni Mitchell, 'The Magdeline Laundries', from The Chieftains album, *Tears of Stone*

drudgery, *n.* The long, unremitting, unrewarding work done by teenage girls in cheap bed-and-breakfast lodgings, particularly those that trade under the name of Samarkand.

drudge, *n.* The name given to the girls who do such work.

The Blue Notebook

still nothing

The work at Samarkand was pure drudgery, because we did nearly everything 'by hand'. Sophie said it was a wonder our hands were still so young and lovely-looking, after everything they had been through. They ought to look like a hundred-year-old's hands. They ought to look like Lil's hands.

There was no dishwasher, though there was a washing machine and a vacuum cleaner. But I would have loved to see a machine (apart from a girl) that could make beds. Or serve breakfasts. There was a toaster to make the toast, but someone still had to pop the bread into the toaster, and it was usually me.

On Saturdays I worked for money in a cafe, to save up for university – I was planning to work there full-time after my exams were over. The cafe was called the Dancing Goanna, and it was across the river on the wild side of town, where students and hippies hung out. The tables and chairs were old laminex and vinyl ones, and none of them matched. There was a courtyard with a long, messy garden behind it, full of long grass, nasturtiums trailing orange and yellow flowers, and bok choy gone to seed. The place looked like the country. There was a lot of rusty galvanised iron everywhere and unpainted timber walls, but people didn't care because the coffee was good and strong and the atmosphere was so genuinely daggy it was fashionable.

After work, on a Saturday soon after Sophie had come home from hospital, I didn't feel like heading straight back to Samarkand, so I wandered the streets for a while. I longed so much for a life somewhere else. I thought of all the people who must live in rooms filled with light and books in famous cities. The stone buildings would be shrouded with mist, and the lights on the water mesmerising and magical. In a place like that, you could stay up all night and watch the oyster-coloured dawn creep slowly over ancient buildings, and breakfast with people as beautiful and mysterious as you were. People like the ones Anaïs Nin wrote about in her journal.

That day, the sky was a flat blue, and enormous. The streets were so still and the colours so washed-out that my body felt hollow. In the empty main street, a few people went in and out of the pub and the video store, or hung about aimlessly in front of the milk bars. I walked past the alleyway that led to Hope Springs. The shop was closed and shuttered, and I thought of all those books dwelling there in the dark, sleeping their time away till the shop was opened up again. I thought about the boy I'd met there. He had such an aura of exoticism about him, of having known other places and even other times.

That afternoon my life seemed particularly dull. I spied

a beautiful woman driving somewhere fast in a sleek car, and a feeling of such quiet desperation came over me that I wanted to cry.

Walking back past Samarkand, I noticed how the bright afternoon light revealed it as unbearably shabby, all its blemishes laid bare for the world to see. I tried to go past with an impartial eye, as though I didn't live there, and came at last to a small bridge that crossed the river a little way along the street, just before it became the country.

Here, a Landcare group had planted rainforest trees to blend in with the original vegetation that had been left accidentally uncleared. As I crossed the bridge I glimpsed a fox – white muzzle and orange fur, lean and mangey – as it darted back into the trees to avoid a passing car. Its hunted expression imprinted itself on my mind.

I walked a little way into the trees, where the earth showed bare under the damp fallen leaves. Somewhere here lived a fox, with a den, and perhaps a mate and cubs. A fox is an alien animal, unwanted and despised, and its fear of people is well-founded. Once I'd seen the ancient remains of a fox – a few scraps of fur and crushed bones – lying on the surface of a road. Foxes reminded me of a childhood book, *The Little Prince*, which I still read sometimes when I was feeling nostalgic for those days. When the little prince meets the fox, the fox says that if the little prince tamed him, it would be as if the sun came to shine on his life. The sound of his footsteps would be different from all the others. 'If you tame me, then we shall need each other.'

I sat down under the trees near the river, and shivered in the cool, damp shade, thinking about the fox, and about taming and needing. I felt like being gloomy and moody and miserable.

Late in the afternoon I made my way back to Samarkand. It had been grand once; now it was just a shabby old house. It was full of shadows and damp, dark corners; the boards creaked at night like an arthritic old lady, and every winter morning the condensation under the verandah roofs dripped onto the floor, making everything wet. Sometimes I thought I would never escape from it, and was doomed to live there *for ever and ever*, like a trapped princess in a fairy tale.

When I got back, Lil was in the kitchen puffing on a cigarette and thinking about putting on the dinner. Breakfast was the only meal we served to the guests. They had to make their own arrangements for dinner. Many of them ate take-aways or went to the pub, though there was a kitchenette for their use tucked away on a side verandah. Dinner for us was meant to be a family occasion, without the intrusion of business, though often guests came knocking on the kitchen door, wanting something.

'Hello, darlin',' said Lil. 'Have a good day?'

I didn't bother to reply.

Lil took a plate of mince out of the fridge and stubbed out her cigarette. She squirted red wine from a cask into a glass, took a sip, and put it down on the table. Lil did everything that was bad for you, and her breathing was often laboured.

'You *know* Sophie won't eat *that*!' I told her. The meat squatted there like a minced toad, seeping blood. Sophie had been a vegetarian, of sorts, for a long time.

'She won't even notice a little bit of meat in the sauce. She could do with some building up,' said Lil dismissively.

I was *starving*. I reached into the cupboard for the jar of almonds that Lil kept to put on top of fruit cakes, tipped out a handful and crammed them into my mouth.

'Why did I have to get a name like Kate?' I said, sounding as sulky as I possibly could. 'Why couldn't I have a name like Persephone, or Aphrodite, or Cassandra?'

Lil *still* hadn't started cooking the dinner. She kept puttering round the kitchen with her little *old-lady* steps, wiping down something here, moving something else there.

'Kate is such a – *clunky* name. It just sort of falls down – clunk – like a brick. Or a cow-pat. *Kate*. It doesn't have any mellifluous syllables. It doesn't *flow*.'

Why couldn't I have been called something like Anaïs? I wondered. If I had a name like Anaïs I couldn't help but be a writer. It would be in my blood.

'When you were seven you wanted to be called Hepzibah,' said Lil. 'Where would you be if I'd gone along with you then? Stuck with it.' Lil took the jar of nuts from me and put it back into the cupboard.

I attacked a bowl of grapes, picking them from the stems savagely. I should have made Lil call me Hepzibah. There was a woman named Hepzibah in a book I'd read at the time. Hepzibah Green. She was lovely – warm and motherly and almost a witch as well.

The phone in the hall rang. Lil was in the middle of chopping a large onion, so I flung myself from the room to answer it. I could feel myself doing the flinging, feeling ridiculous, but unable to stop myself.

It was for Lil of course; one of her friends. 'Lil! It's for you!' I yelled. Lil waddled out and plopped down in a chair next to the phone, a freshly lit cigarette dangling from her fingers.

'What's up?' she said, into the receiver.

Lil knew thousands of old women who were always coming round and sitting with her in the kitchen, smoking and playing cards and cackling about everything far into the night. The place became thick with smoke and raucous laughter. They seemed never to want to go home, and their voices were so loud that the sound drifted up to my room and stopped me from sleeping. I'd toss and turn with the pillow over my head and finally race down to the kitchen and tell them all to be quiet. I knew that now she would sit on the phone for hours, and dinner wouldn't get cooked, and I would *starve to death*.

I crashed a large pot down on the stove, splashed in some olive oil, and tossed in the onion Lil had partially chopped.

'Oh, Gawd.' (Lil often called on Gawd. It was her fault that Sophie and I had no sense of blasphemy: we had been brought up without Religion.)

'Oh, I am so sorry. What can I say?'

Those cooks on television are always going on about how important it is that food is made with *luurve*. But I think a lot of the food in the world must be made with irritation. Every soothing sentence that Lil crooned to her friend just made me more and more annoyed.

'Look, you cry, love, it's probably just what you need. Nothing wrong with crying.'

I tipped the toad into the pot where it sat wetly on top of the onion and oil, and allowed it to slowly seethe in its own juices.

'Oh, you poor, poor love.'

I found a soggy tomato lurking at the back of the fridge, and lined it up on the bench with a limp bunch of celery (Why does some celery insist on smelling like cat pee?), a couple of flaccid carrots, a disgruntled-looking capsicum and an eggplant that begged to be put out of its misery.

'I know, I know.'

When I'd chopped the vegetables into an abject heap, I tossed them in, along with a large tin of tomatoes. I added a spurt of tomato paste, a handful of herbs, a splash of soy sauce, and gave it a stir.

'Oh, I know how you're feeling.'

I gave a final stir and clanged on the lid, to make sure Lil would hear it.

'Children. They just break your heart.'

Then I walked heavily down the hallway, past Lil waving her cigarette around and making soothing noises into the phone. On the verandah I was accosted by a guest, a woman in one of those shapeless linen dresses that I really hate. 'Excuse me,' said the woman, 'but there's a frog in the downstairs toilet bowl.'

I stood there for a moment as if gobsmacked, so that she'd know that the frog in the toilet bowl was not my responsibility.

'I just live here,' I said, pleased with the way I'd maintained my dignity, 'I'm not the maid!' and kept going to my room, which is on the top floor at the back, where the wrap-around verandah comes to a full stop. It was a small room looking out into thick trees, a quiet, gloomy space as secretive as the place where I had seen the fox.

I liked it that way, as I am nocturnal myself, with pale skin and large light-seeking eyes.

On the verandah outside my room was an old sofa covered by a bedspread to stop its innards from leaking everywhere. It was the place where I sat, especially at night, and looked out into the trees and palms that pressed against the back of the house, and listened to the fruit bats squabbling over blossom and berries.

I grabbed Anaïs Nin's *Journals* and took it out to the sofa. There was just enough light to see by (if Lil had come past she'd have squarked, 'Oh, lovey, you'll *roon* your eyes!'), and I lay for a long while and looked into Anaïs Nin's face. Anaïs Nin looked back at me. I couldn't believe that she was dead, because when you read her book it sounded as though she'd just written it.

I opened it at the beginning, and read the start again. *Winter, 1947. Acapulco, Mexico.* Anaïs Nin is lying in a hammock with her diary open on her knees, and she has no desire to write. Her senses overwhelm her – the sun, the leaves, the shade, the warmth. She is experiencing perfection.

I turned again to the face on the cover. She was quite *old* – forty-four – when this particular journal was started. Lying in the hammock in Mexico, feeling no need to portray or preserve what she is experiencing, Anaïs Nin feels in full possession of her own body. Everything is pleasure.

I couldn't help wondering if Lil was off the phone yet, and if the dinner was ready. I was hungry, and couldn't wait any longer. On my window sill sat five pears, Josephines (the best variety: the nicest name, compared to William or Bartlett or Bosc, and the best shape, like a plump drop of water). They glimmered in the twilight. I liked to keep fruit in my room in case of sudden hunger. They were a happiness of pears, sitting there in a row.

I chose two and took them around the verandah to Sophie's room. It was at the front, overlooking the park and the river, open to the light and the air and the sky. Sophie was lying in bed on her side with Anastasia latched on and sucking. It was the perfect position for reading, and Oscar Wilde lay open on the bed beside her; her eyes were fixed on it.

I handed her a pear and she took it without looking up from her book. Biting into my Josephine, I found that it was perfect: juicy, sweet and spicy at the same time. Sophie also made greedy inroads into hers, and a splash of juice fell onto Anastasia's face. She wiped it away and continued reading. She finished her pear, core and all, and dropped the stalk onto the open page of *The Collected Works of Oscar Wilde*.

I started to tell her about the fox, about the look on its face that I'd seen before it fled. But Sophie had fallen asleep, quite suddenly, as she often did these days, her glasses crooked on her face. Anastasia was asleep too, her mouth lolling open, her hands folded into fists.

The Red Notebook

From the Oxford Dictionary:

exo – from the Greek, meaning *outside*

exotic – meaning 1: (of plants, words, fashions):
introduced from abroad. 2: striking and attractive through
being colourful or unusual

exotic things that come to mind: mangoes (not yet in
season but Sophie and I are already dreaming of them);
the boy in the bookshop (whom I may never see again)

The Journals of Anaïs Nin
Summer 1953, New York
Anaïs dreams of the evening and what it will bring at
twilight; it is the hour she loves best, and it also saddens
her. She ceases the day's efforts, she bathes, and dresses
for some event. She loves this time best, the 'in-between
hours', the only moment when she exists alone.

The Pillow Book of Sei Shonogon

The Pillow Book is written by a woman who was a lady-in-waiting at the Court of the Japanese Empress in tenth-century Japan. She writes down all the things that attract, displease her etc. in daily life. She seems to have been quite promiscuous – her lovers discreetly steal away from her in the early hours of the morning. She's always writing lists. For example, Poetic Subjects (Arrowroot???), and Things That Cannot be Compared (summer and winter, night and day, and she also puts in this category) 'When one has stopped loving somebody, one feels that he has become someone else, even though he is still the same person'. Also Hateful Things ('One is about to be told an interesting piece of news and a baby starts crying.' I'd hate that too!). But the bit I like best is under When a Woman Lives Alone. She says that when a woman lives alone her house should be extremely dilapidated, the mud wall should be falling to pieces, and if there is a pond it should be overgrown with water-plants. She hates a woman's house when it is clear that she has scurried about with a knowing look on her face, arranging everything just as it should be . . . (She would love Samarkand, where nothing is arranged as it should be!)

The Yellow Notebook

The girl with the yellow hair, who wears the charcoal suit and high heels to work in the day, relaxes at night in her kimono and bare feet, lying on an old sofa. After drinking the mint tea, she makes herself a mushroom omelette for dinner. She eats a mango afterwards, licking away the sticky juice that runs over her wrists and down her arm. She loves this time of the day, when she can relax, and be alone.

Now she reads (the luxury of it!) till the small hours of the morning. Books fill the shelves that line the walls of her room; she has so many they spill over into piles on the floor and over the coffee table; they are stacked up beside the sofa, so she has only to reach out her hand and it touches a book.

The books are many and various. There are new books, with clean, shiny covers and crisp pages, and there are old books, rare books, with beautiful dustjackets and intriguing inscriptions inside. Their pages are beautiful in a different way from the clean, sweet-smelling white pages of the new books – these old books have thick, cream-coloured paper, browned on the edges, some as crisp as a perfectly fried egg. They all smell different – of rich, old spices, or deep green forests, earthy and damp. They evoke long-forgotten rooms and other lives.

She reads and reads, occasionally picking up a piece of Turkish delight and savouring the intense flavour, which is like a thousand red rose petals crushed into one sweet, sticky little cube.

Suddenly restless, she goes to the window. There, in the garden, is the glint of the eyes that she sees each night. She fetches a bowl and some milk, and goes outside and sets it down just beyond the window. She retreats, and waits.

Cautiously, an animal approaches. It is a fox. It laps at the milk, poised for flight at any moment. She doesn't move; she just watches it.

I went again to Hope Springs, hoping to see the
boy I'd met there; the boy whose name I didn't know.
Actually, he wasn't a boy, not like the boys I was friends
with at school (Jason with his saxophone, Zed who was
crazy about cooking Italian food). He was a man, though a
young one, and he had an interesting air of having lived in
the world – the huge, ocean-sized world that existed beyond
Lismore. Perhaps that's why I was so drawn to him.

I'd never had a boyfriend – never wanted one – though
Jason used to come round to play the saxophone for me,
and he kissed me once when he was dropping me off after a
party, but I ignored it, pretending afterwards that it hadn't
happened. His mouth had felt strange against mine, too soft,
and it made me think of jelly-like sea-creatures.

If the boy wasn't there this time, I thought, that would
be it. I would never darken the bookshop door again.

And he wasn't there. Instead there was a man (not
young at all, and very whiskery) shelving a box of books
that someone had left at the doorway of the shop like an

abandoned baby. The shop was a kind of home for books, and they would stay there until someone came to take them away and love them. Some of them would probably stay there forever, they were so tattered and unattractive, but Hope Springs had a policy of turning nothing away. Every single time I went to the shop, I found a book I liked the look of, and I bought it. Even though I mightn't read them just yet, I liked to have them stored up against possible periods of booklessness in my life.

It was worth going to Hope Springs just for the books, and I thought I'd have to break my resolve not to go there any more. I despaired of seeing the bookshop boy ever again.

I finally met him because I liked to travel across town using the laneways. I enjoyed their narrowness, and the way they slid past the backs of the houses so you could peer into the back yards. The back is the part of the house that people don't expect you to see and it is always more individual and interesting.

Entering a laneway on foot (my bicycle out of action with a flat tyre), I saw that the boy I'd met at Hope Springs had just stepped into it at the opposite end. We walked down the lane with each other in full view, our eyes full of boldness, and reached the middle of the lane at the same time.

We halted.

The boy smiled. I smiled. 'Hello', we said, and stood there smiling at each other.

'I'm Persephone,' I told him. I was always trying to get people to call me by more glamorous names but they never did, probably because they were used to me being plain old Kate.

'Alex,' he said, and held out his hand.

He had a soft line of down on his upper lip, and I couldn't stop staring at it. Sophie was always telling me I shouldn't stare at people so much, it disconcerted them. But Alex wasn't at all disconcerted. 'I was just on my way home,' he said, and gestured to a fence covered with choko vines. 'Do you want to come in?'

Alex lived in a garage in the back yard of an old house, and it smelt faintly of old car oil. Down one end there were shelves filled with ancient paint tins and mower parts and jars of rusty nails. The other end of the room was Alex's domain. It was inexpressibly bare and neat, with the kind of neatness that sets your teeth on edge like sucking lemons. This may have been because he possessed barely anything at all. Of all the things that are to be possessed in the world, Alex had almost none.

The inventory of Alex's belongings that first day was as follows:

a single bed with a clean, faded cover tucked tightly over it

a bench along one side of the room on which sat

a cup

a plate

a bowl

a bread knife

a fork

a two-burner gas camping stove

a plastic washing-up bowl

a kettle

an onion that had seen better days

and a pile of newspapers.

And also, and most interestingly, on the other side of the room, there was a small table on which sat:

an electric typewriter and

a new ream of copying paper.

'Could I offer you a cup of something, Persephone?' he said. In the midst of this bare-faced lack of possessions, Alex was the most attentive host possible.

'Please do,' I said. 'What do you have?'

'Well, there's mint tea, or hot water. Or cold if you'd prefer.'

'Mint tea would be perfect.' I sat on the bed because there was nowhere else to sit.

Alex went out through the door at the end of the garage with the kettle and reappeared with a handful of freshly picked mint leaves and the kettle full of water. He chopped up the leaves, sprinkled them into the cup and, when the water boiled, poured it over them.

'Sugar?'

He reached up to a shelf and took down a small Vege-mite jar.

'How much? Mint tea is better if it's sweet,' he suggested.

'Definitely. You decide.'

Using the blade of the knife, Alex transferred rather a lot of sugar to the cup, and stirred. He handed it to me and I took a sip. It tasted refreshingly of the Near (or was it the Far?) East, of shaded courtyards and oases and dancing girls. Alex sat down beside me and, since there was only one cup, I handed it to him so he could have some too. 'I really prefer coffee,' he said, 'But I'm trying to wean myself off it.'

Sometimes it is easier to feel intimate with strangers than with people that you know well. The more you know about someone, the more you realise how much about them you don't know. With a stranger it is like the innocent meeting of two souls; you float on a warm swell of good feeling. But you can't sit there and say nothing. Inevitably, the knowing process begins.

'You type?' I asked, glancing over at the typewriter.

'Badly. Two fingers.' Alex smiled.

'So – why do you have a typewriter?'

'I'm trying to write a novel.' Alex gestured for me to keep possession of the mint tea. He got up and walked over to the typewriter. A sheet of blank paper had been rolled into the carriage, but there was nothing written on it. He leaned over and took out the paper; it curled up at each end.

'Are you having any success?' I wondered.

'None whatsoever.'

The words hung gloomily in the bare room like a small dark cloud.

'I have writer's block.'

'What does that mean, exactly? Or even approximately?'

I waited for his reply. Sophie had told me that you shouldn't always let words rush in to fill empty conversational spaces.

At last Alex said, 'It means I can't write. I can't even make a start. Something stops me from putting words down. I sit at the typewriter and nothing comes. It's like being paralysed.'

Alex stared at the blank sheet in his hand. He turned it over and looked at the other side of the paper as if contemplating an object he'd never before encountered, or in case words had magically appeared there in his absence.

Pages are such daunting things. Unwritten on, they are so pure, so white, so unsullied, like freshly fallen snow.

So silent.

Who would dare to put footprints there? I felt that I, for one, wouldn't be able to take even one step. I'd fall face forward into the snow and lie there, spreadeagled, my very breath muffled by that weighty silence.

I thought about my notebooks, especially the red one, which I'd had no trouble beginning at all. That was because it wasn't real writing – just random thoughts, and quotations, and notes about books I was reading. I never really expected anyone to ever read it, despite my reference to posterity at the beginning.

I stared at Alex's blank page. This was a different matter. A page where he hoped he might write something significant. A whole novel. Neither of us spoke. We sat silently and pondered the enormous task of filling page after page with print, when it was so difficult to make even the first mark.

Marjorie lived on a broad, quiet street lined with shady fig trees, in a house framed by a large garden with a perfectly manicured lawn, and tasteful shrubs and flowers. The house had been built in the 1930s and her parents had renovated it to retain its period character. A deep front verandah led to a double living room with sliding-glass doors dividing it down the middle.

I always ran up the front steps and called, 'Coo-ee!' at the open front door to let Marjorie know I was there, then bounded down the hallway to where Marjorie sat in the panelled dining room with her books spread about over the table. Her parents were always at work during the week, and Marjorie liked to study in the dining room rather than her bedroom, as the house seemed less lonely that way. She was an only child. Her mother was an accountant, an almost unbelievably beautiful woman with long auburn hair. She drove a restored 1965 Holden (pale green, very shiny), and had a trick of being able to remove her bra without taking off her top. She did this every day, in the living room, when she arrived home from work, so Marjorie said.

I slipped into a chair opposite Marjorie. Her notebooks were filled with indecipherable squiggles and symbols – she studied a hideously high level of maths and physics. Marjorie wanted to be a doctor, like her father. 'Tea?' she asked, removing her glasses and looking at me gratefully. I had probably arrived just in the nick of time to prevent her brain exploding. We went to the kitchen, where Marjorie put on the kettle and set out bone china cups and plates.

Marjorie had slipped through the fabric of time and was really from another era – the 1940s, say, or the 1950s. She hadn't been born at all. For one thing, her parents would have been far too busy to give birth to her. I imagined that she had skipped into her parents' kitchen one day at the age of five or six, carrying a little suitcase and humming a tune, and had been there ever since.

She was the loveliest-looking girl I had ever seen, small and slim, with black hair cut short and curled around her face, alabaster skin, and clear, intensely blue eyes. The sort of girl you just wanted to look and look at, she was so pretty. She wore crisp cotton pastel frocks with sprigs of flowers, and sandals.

When she wasn't studying maths and physics, Marjorie baked cakes. She did it with scientific precision, weighing the ingredients on a scale and sifting the flour from a good height so it would be beautifully aerated. She wore an apron when she baked and, in their cream and green renovated 1930s kitchen, she could have been someone in an old-fashioned advertisement.

That day, she had baked a sponge and filled it with jam and cream. She poured the tea from a silver teapot and I sliced the cake. Marjorie ate delicately, with a cake fork. Lil always said that I fell upon my food like a starving man, and that day was no exception. I picked up my slice and took enormous greedy mouthfuls. There were not many moments of the day when I was not starving hungry.

Marjorie and I had been friends since primary school. Both of us, in different ways, were unlike the other girls at school, so it suited us to stick together. For me, Marjorie was a *safe* friend; with her there were none of the passions and uncertainties that characterised Sophie's relations with Carmen and Rafaella.

I enjoyed the calmness of being with her. I enjoyed her quiet and ordered household in contrast to my own, which was so often intruded on by strangers.

'Have you been studying?' Marjorie asked.

'Not much,' I said, feeling slightly guilty.

'Well, what else have you been up to? The exams aren't that far off, you know.'

Furtively, remembering my recent encounter with Alex, I shrugged.

'You needn't look as if I'm interrogating you.'

'On the way here today I drank mint tea with a Russian prince,' I blurted out.

'Of course! What else is there to do, on a Monday morning?'

'But really,' I said. The sweet taste of his exotic tea still seemed to be in my mouth.

'What's his name?'

'Alex.'

I hesitated. 'I told him my name was Persephone.'

'After all, that *is* your name.'

'He's a writer.'

'Really? What's he written?'

'Nothing. He told me he's writing a novel, but he has writer's block.'

'Very painful.'

I stared at Marjorie across the table; we started to giggle. I felt an instant pang of disloyalty, to be laughing about Alex with Marjorie so soon after meeting him, and the mint tea, and everything. I had meant to keep him as my secret. Now, here I was, blabbing it at the first opportunity.

But Alex did look like a Russian prince. Perhaps he was one. Anything was possible.

The Red Notebook

I am sitting in the dark in my fig tree and my bottom is icy cold. I am discovering that you can write without seeing what you are writing and that is somehow very liberating, though it's bound to be indecipherable.

Behind me is the river. The water glimmers in the moonlight, and it looks better than it does in the daylight, when it is oily-looking and sometimes muddy and you can see the scrappy weeds along the banks. My nostrils are cold, and I can smell where the weeds along the roadside have been mown today by the Council tractor.

When I was a child I considered this tree my second home. Actually, it was my real home, because it was all mine, and it was where I felt most myself. Only Marjorie was ever invited in. Sophie used to sit on the ground at the bottom and call up to me. I have never told anyone this, but I used to pretend that I lived here with my mother and father. When I got home from school my mother was waiting with a glass of milk and biscuits just like old-fashioned Moms in American movies and my father was in a chair smoking a pipe.

This tree is vast, like a cathedral or an ocean liner. When I was little I had parts of it all mapped out into kitchen and bedrooms and living room, all connected by the passageways of broad branches.

But I intended to write about the here and now, not the past. I am staring out through the leaves at Samarkand. My tree is in darkness, but lights shine out from Samarkand as from a city on a distant shore. It is another country there.

There is a burst of loud music from Sophie's room. She is playing her current favourite song, 'Because the Night', by Patti Smith, very loudly. It's a song that breaks my heart because of the way the music makes a pattern of such longing, one note against another. I know that Sophie longs for Marcus, though she would not tell anyone, and this is the reason she plays the song.

The music has stopped suddenly but I can still hear it in my head. Anastasia begins to cry, so mournfully I want to go to her. Anastasia loves the song too, and hates the silence. Perhaps the song reminds her of her father, though she has never met him. But there is a little bit of him in her, so she must know him in some way – the parts of her that are like him call to him.

Two guests are sitting on the steps smoking – I can see the twin eyes of their cigarettes gleaming in the dark. And from the lower verandah a harmonica starts up, a heartfelt, melancholy tune. The harmonica player is a man from somewhere in the north of England, and he has been staying this past week. He's an oldish man, and I believe that he's either severely missing his homeland or pining for a long-lost lady love. (He actually used this term 'lady love' when he saw two of the other guests canoodling. 'Oh, to have a lady love,' he said, longingly.)

The tune he's playing is 'Dirty Old Town', and it's a tune full of longing. A lot of the people who come here are longing for something and looking for something (I know I have used too many 'longings' – Ms M, my English teacher, would probably tell me to use another word). Sometimes I think the house might fill with so much other people's longing that it will float away like a hot-air balloon.

Now Sophie walks out onto the verandah with Anastasia in her arms, looks out into the darkness, and goes back into her room again.

Lil comes onto the verandah and shakes a white tablecloth out over the edge of the railing. It floats up and down three times, and it seems so slow that all time is suspended. She catches it in her arms, turns, and goes inside.

Now all the lights in the house are out, except for one, the welcoming light next to the nameplate next to the front door. SAMARKAND, it says, though I can't read it.

The Yellow Notebook

Written in my room with the aid of electric light. What I have learned: If you want to be able to write with facility, handicap yourself first.

Music: 'Possessed', by Crowded House

The Girl with the Yellow Hair:

She is in the happy position of liking every bit of her life. She likes her work, something that people are not always lucky enough to do.

Each weekday morning, after a breakfast of sourdough toast and cumquat jam and strong coffee, she takes the train into the city, where, in a street lined with green linden trees, she works in an office situated in an old house.

It is a publishing house. At first, when she came here, and found that the *house* part was literally true, she was astonished, because she thought that something as important as a publisher would be in one of those glass and steel tower blocks. But this one is in an actual house, a huge old terrace that goes up and up, rooms everywhere, and inside it are people (mostly women) busy with the business of publishing books.

As yet, she doesn't have an office of her own. It is her job to do all the everyday things – opening mail, clipping reviews, answering the phone – but in between times she is allowed (no – not allowed – *exhorted*) to read the manuscripts, especially the ones that are to be published, so that she can get her eye in for what is good. And the rest of the time she reads the books that have already been published, and sit in rows on shelves, just waiting to be read. This, she thinks, must be heaven.

It is a happy place to work. She closes her eyes sometimes and thinks she can feel all that industry going on around her – all those minds intent on books – all the words floating round the building. Words literally float round the building sometimes too, because once a week all the people who work there gather in one of the larger rooms at lunchtime and sing, in parts, so that their voices blend together most harmoniously . . .

And they lie about on the floor sometimes, these people who work with books, reading or talking to each other. Just lie about among the manuscripts, which sit in piles on tables and shelves, great white stacks of them, with rubber bands about them. In the absence of beds (which is the proper place to read), they just stretch out on the floor and

(O God now Lil wants me for something!)

I had still recorded nothing in the Blue Notebook, which I had come to think of as my memory notebook. I did remember things of course. How can you go through childhood without a single, solitary memory?

I could, for instance, have written in the Blue Notebook:

In bed with Lil and Sophie at Samarkand. Lil snoring, the sag of the mattress tilting me towards her heavy warmth. Sophie on my other side, tossing and muttering in her sleep. I'm drowsily awake, my head under the covers, breathing in the sweet musty mingled odours of our skins. Curled into Lil's back, one hand on her shoulder. Her soft flesh. My other hand, fingering her nightie. Feeling the threads of cotton and noticing the difference in texture between skin and fabric.

The verandah door open to an early summer's day. The sound of someone – something walking across the wooden floor.

A cry. Harsh and raucous. Enough to curdle blood. To wake the dead.

secret scribbled notebooks by secret scr

Lil sits bolt upright, throws back the sheet.

Two crows fly from the room. As black as sin. The wind of their wings, cutting the air like a sword. Beaks sharp as spears. Cries like black ice.

'I'm not dead yet!' Lil calls.

Sophie wakes and murmurs; is asleep again.

Lil lies back down. 'The hide of them,' she says. 'As if they were ready to pluck out my eyes. But I'm not dead yet. Not yet.'

Lil's hair had been the same unchanging colour since we'd known her, and her colour was Jet Black. For years now, it had been our job to help her dye it. We fought about whose turn it was (*'Bags not mine!'*). It was a dreary ritual: the chair in the bathroom, the towel round her shoulders, the gloves, the goo, the combing through, the waiting, the washing out, the whole chemical stink of it.

For the dyeing process, Lil wore a nylon slip, and the straps cut into her rounded, mottled shoulders. The features on her face were blurring with age, growing less defined day by day, so that sometimes I feared that she was becoming less and less Lil, and more and more just an Old Person. She had a peculiar smell of old sweat mixed with talcum powder.

She had worn her hair the same way for years, done up in a french roll. I could see when I dyed it that the real colour was pure white, and wished Lil would let just one streak of that proper colour grow out; it would make a spectacular black-and-white effect. Sophie hankered to cut Lil's hair in a short, spiky style, but Lil wouldn't have it.

Lil complained that we spent far too much time reading, but she had set a bad example. When we were little she was always sneaking off to where no one could find her and reading books and eating chocolates. She treated the guests like children that she needed to take a break from for her own sanity. I used to find her in her favourite sofa on the back verandah, a book and a ciggie in her hands and lollies in her pockets. 'Is that you, lovey?' she'd call: I knew it wasn't me she was hiding from. Lil would pull me onto the sofa for a cuddle, stroking the curls away from my face. I'm ashamed to say that I now avoided a cuddle from Lil – her puckered red lips, the folds of her skin, made me shudder.

It was Lil who taught us to read, so it was her fault that we were so addicted to it. But I thought that I must have been born able to read, the learning was so effortless. Lil would take us on either side of her and we'd sit there, eagerly looking at the book as she read to us.

'I can read!' Sophie announced out of the blue one day, standing in the kitchen with a half-eaten apple in her hand.

'Sez who?' said Lil.

'Sez me!' (hands on hips and chin stuck out defiantly).

'Go on . . . who taught you?'

'I taught myself!'

'Well, read something to me.'

'Lan-choo Tea!' (pointing at the packet).

'Very good. And what does this say?'

'Kellogg's Cornflakes!'

'Can you read books?'

'I can especially read books!'

Sophie's second day of school: I go to our shared room in the middle of the morning and see a movement behind the curtain. A face appears. 'It's me!'

'I ran away,' Sophie tells me. 'School's boring!'

We sit behind the curtain together. The curtain is red and voluminous and hides us pretty well. Or so we think. Anyway, the girl who's meant to be looking after me while Lil gets on with the work never worries about what I'm doing. Sophie and I have a stash of picture books with us, and paper and textas for drawing with, and Sophie's school lunch. It's a complete and perfect world there behind the curtain.

We peel apart the sandwiches and lick the butter and Vegemite off first, poring stickily over the pictures in the books. We eat the cream biscuits from Sophie's playlunch. Later, I sneak to the kitchen and fetch a fistful of crackers, and we suck the salt away and nibble the crimped edges. Sophie reads to me in a whisper.

But then the school rings Lil, and we are discovered.

Sophie did end up going to school almost every day, so I got Lil's lap to myself. I always listened closely when Lil read to me, and pulled her up when she got a word wrong. Lil thought I just knew the book by heart, but I knew how to read long before I let on to Lil that I could. I'd read along under my breath, but I was caught out one day when Lil stopped reading and I continued on, my lips moving almost soundlessly, my eyes following the text. 'Why, you little monkey!' said Lil. 'You can read for yourself, can't you?'

But that didn't stop Lil reading to me, as I'd feared she would. The books she read were old ones she'd had around for years and years; I now see that they must have belonged to Lil's son, Alan. They were about trains and boats with faces and feelings who learned valuable life lessons. A train called Tootle had to learn to *stay on the rails no matter what*. A boat named Scuffy sailed off down the river till he reached the sea, only to be snatched up at the last moment by his owner and returned to sailing in the bathtub. Another train tried and tried until he reached the top of a steep hill. 'I think I can. I think I can,' he said. And of course, he could.

I enjoyed the pictures of Tootle when he was off the rails the best. He romped through fields of flowers with blossoms floating in the bowls of soup in his dining car and flowers draped rakishly across his engine. I thought it looked like far more fun off the tracks. And I felt sorry for the little boat who found the sea far too wide for him, because I felt sure that the ocean would be far more exciting than a mere bathtub.

Although Lil loved to read as much as she loved to smoke and drink red wine and play cards with her friends, she treated it as a guilty pleasure that had to be stolen from the imperatives of the day. Sophie and I learned to snatch our reading time as well, and Lil was always onto us for reading when we ought to have been doing something else.

Standing outside my room, she'd call, 'Kate, are you getting ready for school?'

'Kate?'

'KATE!'

'Yes, Lil?'

'I know what you're up to in there! Put down that book! Are you dressed yet?'

'Almost.'

'Well, hurry up about it, madam, or we'll have the police here.'

The police dominated Lil's threats. I imagined uniformed hordes of them, wielding truncheons, swarming up the zig-zag steps of Samarkand and converging on my room where I cowered, half-dressed in singlet and knickers, behind the covers of an open book.

The attraction of reading was that while you were doing it you were somewhere else. I loved feeling with my fingers how much of a book there was left to go – all those pages! – time enough for a satisfactory happy ending to be worked out (because what was the use of a book without a happy ending?). I also liked knowing that the fate of the characters had been already worked out, though I had yet to find out what it was. And people couldn't reach you when you were reading. It was a private experience, the ultimate intimacy, something between you and the book.

We spent our entire childhood reading. We nicked off from school to do it; we did it with torches in the small hours of the morning; we curled up hidden behind curtains; we climbed trees for the express purpose of spending a few more stolen hours with a book, in direct defiance of the police, who never did manage to discover us. It was glorious.

We knew that people didn't like it if you read too much, so it was best not to let on what you were up to. Eventually, we discovered characters far more compelling than little trains and boats with faces, although these vehicles will always have a special place in my heart.

We each discovered the book that became *our* book, the book that spoke to our inner selves, in the very same year. Sophie's book, which she first read at fifteen, was *Anna Karenina*. Mine was *Great Expectations*.

Anna Karenina escaped from a loveless marriage and gave her life to a man who, she finally learned, didn't love her in return. She ended up walking under a train and killing herself.

In *Great Expectations*, a jilted woman, Miss Havisham, spent her whole life in bitterness. She adopted a young girl, and taught her not to love, and so this girl, Estelle, couldn't even love her. And the hero Pip, who fell in love with the girl who couldn't love, learnt that his great expectations could not be supplied by other people, and made his own way in the world.

These later books were not so clear-cut as the stories about the little trains and boats had been. If they taught us anything, they taught us that nothing in life is unambiguous and simple.

The Blue Notebook

Anaïs Nin's honesty in her diaries has prompted me to be
brave in what I write. All right. Here it is. This is my only
memory of my father, and it's a nice memory. I have to admit
that my memory of my father is not a horrible one. If
anything, it gives me too much hope. Because he hasn't come
back yet, has he, this man who seemed to love me so much?

I was two. Or three. Certainly no more than three. And
we'd gone to a wedding somewhere. I don't know where.
And I only have a feeling that it was a wedding. I mean,
I remember a wedding, vaguely.

But what I do remember was this. We were staying at
a motel. It was late at night, and I couldn't sleep. I kept
talking and giggling, and whoever else was there tried to
shoosh me – they thought I'd wake up Sophie. And then a
man – my father – picked me up and put on my swimmers,
and took me out to the motel pool. Everyone else was
asleep. The place was dead quiet. It must have been about
two or three in the morning.

We played for ages in the water. I'd jump in, and he'd catch me. He'd pull me through the water and hold on to me and bounce me up and down. It was wonderful. It really was. I was full of wonder. And all the time there was this sort of quiet laughter between us.

I don't even remember his face properly. Just this particular way of smiling, and the way he . . . *was*. He was quiet and sure of himself. He took a lot of notice of me. Not fussing over me, but noticing how I was feeling. It was just the two of us, and the lights sparkling on the water. Everything shimmered.

And I can remember the next morning, I gave him a present I'd found. It was a tiny stone, from the garden of the motel. Nothing special really, just one of the little white stones they use in landscaping. But I found one that I thought was prettier than the rest, and I picked it up and gave it to him. He lifted me up and kissed me on the cheek. He told me that he'd always keep it.

That is why I have always believed he'll come back. And that's all I have for you, Blue Notebook. I remember nothing else. You are now officially obsolete.

The Red Notebook

Music: Emmylou Harris, 'Orphan Girl'

Now I don't feel like writing a thing

I often wondered where Sophie and I had sprung from, and how we got to be the way we were. Where did my sister get her pale skin and dark hair, I my great height and freckles and wild red mop? A man reeling drunkenly down the street one night saw Sophie and stopped to say, sentimentally, 'Ah, a beautiful Irish face!'

Our name, after all, is O'Farrell. We could have Irish blood; we might never know. But perhaps that was why Sophie developed an affinity for Oscar Wilde. And she soaked up any tale of deprivation, especially if it had an Irish setting. She had read countless books about people brought up with drunken parents, living in the slums of Ireland, without enough to eat and no shoes on their feet, overcoming the odds and living happy and fulfilled lives. When she was at high school she knew practically everything there was to know about the Irish Potato Famine of 1845–50. She worked it up into a speech that won her first place in public-speaking competitions all over the place until

a notebooks 7 secret scribbled notebooks

she was beaten at State level by a girl who gave a speech about the bombing of Dresden.

Sophie has such a grave and sincere face when the occasion demands, that she had her audience wringing their hands in sympathy. The Irish potato famine was a story of mass starvation, of families becoming ill from eating blighted potatoes, of incredible loss of life and untold suffering. She'd relate the story of a man named Courtney, who was obliged, in his pitiable state, to *depend on cabbage for several days to support existence*, till death, *more merciful than his own rulers, came to his rescue.*

Sophie opened a bag of chocolate drops and reached for a supermarket catalogue that had fallen out of a newspaper onto her bed. Flicking through it, she said, with her mouth full of chocolate, 'If you had to choose just five items from this catalogue to feed you for an entire week, what would you choose?'

She often played this game with me; I couldn't imagine what premonition of impending starvation or doom had driven her to invent it. But this was a game Sophie took seriously, so I considered my options carefully.

The 5-kilogram bag of potatoes was top of my list. That which kept body and soul together for Irish peasants was good enough for me. I also chose a 3-kilogram bag of oranges (Vitamin C), a large packet of powdered milk (protein and calcium), a bulk pack of lamb chops (iron, protein), and some broccoli.

How much does a human being need in order to survive?

How much in the way of food? How much in the way of love?

Or, more importantly, how much can they do without?

We often lay on Sophie's bed and dreamed up imaginary women who had made do with very little in the way of love. There was a woman who existed on a smile she received every day from a man who served her in the general store where she shopped. And another who kept a letter full of ambiguous tender words in her underwear drawer. It was falling apart at the folds, it had been read and re-read so often. Yet another woman remembered a man she passed in the street who glanced at her in a certain way.

All of these women, naturally, had long skirts and long hair done up in old-fashioned hairstyles. They were women from the past. Modern women wouldn't put up with having so little. Would they? *I want a love that is grand and passionate and overwhelming*, Sophie had told me.

No tattered letters in underwear drawers for her.

I had no idea what kind of love I wanted.

And yet Sophie was dreaming her life away. I found a notebook near her bed with the name *Marcus* scrawled over it in elaborate script. She was always half-asleep in the mornings, dreamily mulling over *Anna Karenina*, filling me in on the latest developments while the toast burned.

'We're trying to run a *business* here,' said Lil. 'I just found a pooey nappy sitting on the verandah for people to step in! Can't you at least put them in the covered bucket I gave you, Sophie?'

'But breast-fed babies have such sweet, innocuous poo!' said Sophie.

'Not if the baby isn't yours,' retorted Lil.

I took it upon myself to wash out the nappies every morning, because Sophie somehow never got round to it. I swooshed the yellow shit out of them with the tap and threw them into the machine with a capful of antiseptic bleach, and became very familiar with the inside of the laundry room, propping a book up against the window while I waited for the rinse cycle to finish.

Anastasia was my reward. Out on the verandah she kicked in her bassinette, exercising her legs in preparation for the time when she would stand up and walk. I tickled her toes on the way past to hang the nappies on the line; Anastasia gave me a look that was not yet a smile, but was working up to it. Every morning I made a bee-line for Sophie's room to see how Anastasia had changed overnight. I didn't want to miss one stage she went through.

I didn't know if Sophie would ever go back to her waitressing job. She had never been one for planning her life. When she left school, everyone thought that she should *do* something with herself besides waitressing in a cafe. They assumed that she would go on to university and study literature, she had such a love of it. But Sophie declared she'd had enough of all that during Year 12. A scholar has to read everything, regardless of whether they like it or not. Sophie wanted to read only what she loved; she said she couldn't stomach writing essays any longer. 'Well, someone has to support the novel,' she'd say crossly, if anyone even so much as hinted that she lay about reading too much. One of the teachers at school always asked after her in an anxious and sorrowful way. I wanted to tell her to have *faith*! Because what I thought

Sophie would do was this: she would read and read for years, lying about on her bed and caring for her baby. And then, having absorbed all the Great Literature of the world, she would write a book of her own and it would be wonderful and amaze people.

But now I wasn't so sure. Whatever energy Sophie had seemed to be seeping out of her, day by day.

Sophie would talk to me about imaginary women in love; she would talk to me about books, and quote from them extensively; she would ask me what I would buy to feed myself from the supermarket catalogue, but she wouldn't talk to me about her life. How did she feel about Marcus? Did she feel afraid of bringing up a baby on her own?

Sophie had never confided in me. But ever since she was a child, Sophie had sometimes talked to herself, at night, while she slept. I was glad when I no longer had to share a room with her. Her voice was clear, but I could never make out what she was saying. It was like listening to someone speak in a foreign language. Uncanny, in the immensity of the dark, to listen to her speak and not be able to understand a word.

The Red Notebook

From the dictionary:

chartreuse (shartrerz), a liqueur; pale apple-green colour (another dictionary says clear, light green with a yellowish tinge) – made by **Carthusian** monks

absinth, a strong, bitter, green-coloured aromatic liqueur, made with wormwood, anise and other herbs, with a pronounced licorice flavour

I can't remember if Anaïs Nin drank these things, but I imagine she would have – is it because the word anise reminds me of Anaïs?

The Yellow Notebook

And every night, when the girl gets home from work, she leaves a bowl of milk out for the fox, and watches for it.

It comes slipping through the trees like a shadow, approaching the milk and lapping avidly, its tongue darting in and out, watching her face all the while.

The fox is a little bit of wildness in the intense, tightly packed life of the city; it exists in the wild strip of garden that runs in a thread of green from yard to yard and along to the waste area beside the railway line. She thinks of it as *her* fox, as though she owns it, but she knows there are some things that you can never own.

Alex had told me he'd be at the bookshop the following Friday, and suggested I meet him there. He finished his shift at lunchtime, and while I waited for him, I browsed the shelves and wondered what it was that he wanted to write a novel about. It seemed to me a very ambitious thing to do. So many books had already been written; writing down words with any plan in mind seemed to be asking too much of any ordinary person. This old bookshop, for instance, in a very dull country town, was stuffed with any number of Great Books by the greatest minds of the last couple of hundred years.

I found myself pulling one of these books from the shelf: *Nausea*, by Jean-Paul Sartre. The front cover had a faint undulation, as if it had been left out in the rain, or wept upon copiously (It bore a strange picture by Salvador Dali: a landscape with a hole in it and a partially melted clock reading about four minutes to six.) I opened it and breathed in the scent – it was a typical Old Book. And the words inside – surely these were words I'd want to read sooner or

secret scribbled notebooks   80   secret scr

later. I took it to the table that served as a counter and found some money. 'Ah, Sartre,' said Alex, and nodded in a knowing way. He said the name differently to the way I would have (didn't Sartre rhyme with Frank Sinatra?). He said it with a soft French sound, all but ignoring the last syllable.

I sat on a chair and started reading, and soon the next person on the roster turned up, and we were able to leave. 'The students from the Conservatorium are playing jazz in the park today,' said Alex. 'We could go and listen.'

On the way to the park we approached a street corner where a boy stood selling socialist newspapers. FREE THE REFUGEES said the front page. The boy was far too thin, with a haunted look to him, and he stood with a paper held up in each hand, displaying the headlines. He looked, I thought, as though he'd been impaled there, like Christ on the cross, or an eagle spread out on a barbed-wire fence. People ignored him as they passed by.

'Hey!' said Alex, greeting him with a smile.

'Hey,' he replied. When he smiled, it only exaggerated his leanness.

They exchanged a few friendly words, and Alex took a coin from his pocket and bought a paper.

'I feel ashamed,' Alex said, as we approached the park, 'to live in this country. The way we treat people who come here for refuge. Children should not be locked up. No innocent people should be locked up. I hate what the government is doing in our name.' His words mingled incongruously with the notes of jazz music floating out to us.

It was early spring, and we sat on the grass in front of the band and bathed in the gentle sun. Leaning back on my arms,

I lifted my face to the sky and wriggled my toes, feeling lucky to be alive and free. Alex had expressed serious sentiments, and ones that I agreed with, but my joy in the day, and in being with Alex, could not be suppressed. I am ashamed to say that quite often my feelings are not worthy; when my mind should be on deeper things, I am often quite shallow.

For instance, I am not normally vain, but I must say that I have incredibly beautiful feet. The rest of me is unremarkable, but everything about my feet is simply lovely: their shape – slender and graceful and high-arched; the skin – smooth and unblemished by the freckles that intrude on almost every other area of my body; and my toes are long and perfectly shaped, with nails like charmingly pink little sea-shells.

That day I took off my sandals and displayed my feet for the world to see. I hoped that Alex would see them and admire them, because they were the one thing about me that had achieved a satisfactory level of beauty.

A girl with rings on her toes and in her belly-button took the microphone and sang, *Summertime, and the living is easy* . . .

And I felt that it was. There was nowhere I'd rather have been at that moment than next to Alex in a park on a spring day. With the sun, and the sweet rhythms of the music winding themselves through my body, and lying on the grass with people all around me, and my beautiful feet, and Alex, I felt that I might unfold into an enormous scented blossom. I stretched out my feet again and hoped to catch Alex's eye, but he was absorbed in the girl who was singing. She had a mane of tawny hair, a quizzical expression on her face, and a voice like dark honey.

Then a boy who'd been lying nearby on the grass got to his knees and packed some things into his bag, preparing to leave. Before he stood up, he looked over and said to me, 'Excuse me, but has anyone ever told you that you have really beautiful feet?'

'You look like a Russian prince,' I told Alex, after the band had packed up and we were wandering through the park together.

He wore a black beret that day, and a threadbare silk scarf round his neck, all grey and blue squares. He was graceful and feline and beautiful, with angular cheekbones, and a thoughtful downward curve to his mouth. He took a slim brown cigarette from a packet and lit it.

'That's because I am one,' he said, blowing the smoke away from me. He had a considering, bright-eyed way of looking at me, and a warm and secret smile.

We lay in the shade of a fig tree. I picked up a selection of the small leathery fruits that had fallen to the ground and said, 'Which one do you like best?'

Without hesitation, Alex plucked one from my palm. 'This one,' he said.

'I like that one, too.' I really did. From a collection of almost identical objects I could always choose the most desirable one. I put it in his top pocket and scattered the rest onto the ground.

'Tell me about being a Russian prince.'

He looked away from me for a moment, his eyes narrowed, his attention concentrated inside his head as though picturing a scene, and then turned and looked directly into my eyes. 'My great-great-grandfather was a member of the aristocracy, and during the Revolution he escaped from Russia in a hay-cart,' he said, 'smuggled under the hay by a young peasant girl who later became his wife. They went to England first and later emigrated to Australia.'

Well. It might be true or it might not be. It was so pat that I suspected not, and realised that I hadn't been asking for the truth but for a story, to fit my preconceptions of him. I remembered the stories I had made up throughout my life to explain my lack of visible parents, our relationship to Lil, and our life at Samarkand.

Alex didn't say any more, and I waited for him to elaborate further, or ask about where I had come from, or my family. When people asked this, I found it difficult to explain; I often evaded the question. If the questioner was someone I liked and trusted, I'd say something like, *I don't know who my parents were. My sister and I are orphans, virtually. We were brought up by a woman who isn't even related to us.* But these words always sounded so forlorn, and said nothing about the way Lil was so familiar to me that I could see exactly the particular parts of her – like the creased, loose skin on her elbows – just by thinking about them. Or how I remembered Lil's dimpled skin, soft and mottled like an overripe pear. The way she always called out, 'Is that you, love?' with a hopeful note in her voice when she heard my footsteps after school. Or how recently this had started to annoy me so much that I wanted to snap at her, *Well, who else could it be?*

But Alex said nothing, and I looked at him and thought how beautiful he was. He lay on the grass and put his hands behind his head and his eyes were as bright as a currawong's (but thankfully not yellow). His teeth showed when he talked, rather charmingly white and sharp. He smiled often. I could see that there was passion in him. People often think of passionate people as being all movement and action and histrionics, but Alex was passionate in a quiet way. He glowed, rather than burned.

I longed to know more about him but didn't want to ask too many questions. It had been silly, asking about him being a Russian prince. I hoped to see him again, and again, and that way get to know him.

Alex lay on the ground looking up at the sky. 'I love that intense blue,' he said. 'My grandfather said that the light is so clear here, so bright, after northern Europe. I've never known anything else, but I can imagine different skies, can't you?' He looked across at me, and his face was so full of longing, his appeal to me so plaintive, that I knew this, at least, wasn't a story.

I looked at his hands. Alex had the fine, slender hands that you see on ancient Asian statues. He was at once young and old. When we stood up I noticed that he was exactly the same height as I was. We could look directly into each other's eyes.

'People say I'm too serious,' he said.

'They say I'm too flippant. Is it true,' I asked him, 'about you being a Russian prince?'

'No. I'm not even Russian, let alone a prince. But there was an escape over a border. My grandparents – it was all a long time ago.'

'Can I see you again?' I tried not to appear too eager.

'Of course,' he said. 'Come to the shop, or my place.' He touched me on the arm. 'But where do you live?'

'Somewhere over there,' I told him, vaguely, waving one arm in a generalised direction.

'Oh, I see. Yonder,' he said, nodding and smiling at me.

'Yes. Yonder.'

So we spoke the same language. I wondered if he also looked up dictionaries in his spare time. But I didn't want to put him off entirely. As we parted, I turned at the last moment to call out, 'I live in a place called Samarkand.'

I imagined myself as a bird flying high above the town, seeing us each going our separate ways; I imagined the rusty roof of Samarkand, and the smaller, vine-covered garage where Alex made his home. I thought of all the people in the world converging and separating, meeting and departing, each their own solitary small person.

The Red Notebook

Well, I'm not a court lady in tenth-century Japan, but here is a list:

Things That I Hate About My Sister
   She is maddeningly untidy.
   She is always telling me what she is *going* to do. For instance, today she said that she was going to wash Anastasia's nighties, and then she was going to sweep her room, and then she was going to make cheese on toast for lunch, and then she was going down town to buy some nursing pads because she is sick of leaking all over her clothes (but then again she thought that she might send me to do this!) . . . but she did none of these things, she just lay on the bed and *talked* about it! I snapped at her – 'Well, don't talk about it, just *do* it!' – and she got offended.
   She *snatched* my copy of Anaïs Nin from me (literally – her hand shot out and she grabbed it with such a look of avarice on her face I can't even describe it!) and now she's reading it, and *moaning* that her life will never be like that,

though if you ask me, Anaïs didn't always have such a great time (this is evident when you really get into it).

Sometimes she ignores me when I say something to her (like, *I was in the middle of that book and I'd like it back soon*).

I wonder if Anaïs Nin always did tell the truth, the whole truth and nothing but the truth.

Because people must lie, even in their own diaries, mustn't they?

I was glad I hadn't needed to explain to Alex about Lil and Sophie. It would have been almost impossible, because living with people is somehow inexplicable and subtle, and between us washed a changing tide of emotions that probably had as much to do with the pull of the moon as anything else. After all, aren't we meant to be almost all water?

'What a perfect little darlin',' Lil had said, when Anastasia was born. Lil loved babies and children. She loved dogs, cats, chooks – anything really. Nothing turned her off – the green slime that issued from the noses of small children, the watery eyes and flaky skin of old people (she never counted herself in this category), the slobbery, meaty breath of dogs.

I knew how delighted Lil had been when Anastasia was born, had seen her dancing alone in the kitchen afterwards. But I also knew that Sophie having a baby so early in life had disappointed Lil. She cried when Sophie told her.

'Oh Gawd,' she sobbed. 'You're doing exactly what

I did. Do you think it's going to be easy bringing up a baby on your own? Do you?'

This was a reference to Lil's own son, Alan. Lil had been a single mother, in the days when that was a shameful and unacceptable thing to be. She'd brought up her child on her own, by making the house an aunt had left to her into a boarding house.

But now Alan was dead. He'd died years before, when he was a grown man, not long after Sophie and I came to Samarkand. We never knew him. There were photos of him in Lil's room. He was her 'lovely boy'. Sometimes I saw her holding a picture of Alan in her hands, just gazing at it. Now that we had Anastasia, I knew what it was like to love someone that much.

Sophie had refused to consider an abortion. 'I'll be almost twenty-one when I have it,' she said. 'That's not so young. It's quite old really, compared with some parts of the world and some periods of history. Stop crying, Lil!'

Lil never got used to the way things were done these days. When Lil had had her baby, it was the thing to wear loose dresses like tents that attempted to conceal the bump. Sophie wore clothes that flagrantly emphasised her growing belly – stretchy pants and T-shirts. She swam in a bikini. 'Are you going out like that?' Lil would cry, as the shape of Sophie's burgeoning body was revealed for the world to see. 'People will think it's disgusting!'

Lil's emotions were always close to the surface. She sobbed, cackled with laughter, screamed in pain, at the drop of a hat. She could scare me with her melodramatic approach to life. One night when I was small, Lil had toothache; it was the night of a dreadful storm. The power went off, and

Samarkand was in darkness. I remembered thunder and lightning, the dancing, menacing shadows thrown by candles, and Lil groaning on the tempest-tossed verandah with a handful of painkillers in one hand and a glass of water in the other. I feared that Lil might die before the night was over.

When Sophie was a teenager and became friends with Carmen and Rafaella, Lil used to cry out dramatically at regular intervals, 'Oh, my friends were right! They said I would never be able to handle you two girls when you got older! You are bold, bold girls!'

Being *bold* was the worst accusation Lil could fling at us, and I felt quite insulted by this. I was very quiet and studious, and so was Sophie, really. We lived through books. And that worried Lil, too. 'Oh, my loves,' she'd plead, 'get your noses out of those books and go and get some exercise! Play sport. What about basketball? Have you ever heard of basketball? That's what girls need – not these flippin' . . . books!'

A slice of life from our lives at that time:

Sophie and I cook dinner in the kitchen and Lil looks after Anastasia. The trouble about cooking with Sophie is that all the cooking is left to me while Sophie reads. Sophie's nose is, literally, in a book. Her bum is on a chair, her feet on the rung of the chair next to her, one hand is holding the book, the other rubs the nape of her neck. Her mind is elsewhere.

I place three zucchini on a chopping board on the table next to her, and hand Sophie a knife, which she looks at as if contemplating an entirely original invention that she hasn't before encountered. She begins to chop the zucchini, slowly and laboriously. She slices them lengthways, which is also the way I do it. No one has taught us to slice them this way, we just do. Lil does them in rounds.

We do a lot of things the same way. We will wander up and down a clothes line, pegging things erratically, a shirt here, a sock there, so that the line is dotted with random garments, with lots of gaps in between them. Lil lines up everything neatly in a row.

For the rest of our lives, Sophie and I will share the same way of doing things. Our childhood is a country whose dimensions and geography are known only by us, and it is this which binds us together. We speak a different language there. No one, apart from us, will quite understand exactly how it was. Most families must be this way, an entity to themselves.

I think of our particular childhood as an island, with high, inaccessible cliffs. Waves pound at the foot of the cliffs, sending up a mist of spray. Seabirds, obscured by mist, hover round the cliffs and call in shrill, beseeching voices.

There is no place to land safely. No sandy beaches with a welcome creek running down to it, no palm trees bending in the balmy wind – just cliffs and the crash and roar of waves. The island itself is high and forbidding, containing impenetrable jungle and alligator-infested swamps.

So I understand why Sophie has spent a large part of her life escaping: migrating to other shores, learning the language of others. For a long time she had become a denizen of Carmenandrafaellaland, and I was not allowed to enter. The three of them would gather in Sophie's bedroom, and I would hover outside, listening to their voices making a most welcome and diverting chatter, longing to be asked to join them, until a bare foot casually pushed the door shut on me.

When I arrived home after seeing Alex in the park, I went straight to Sophie's room. Sophie had barely been out of the house since Anastasia was born. She and the baby virtually lived in the bed, which was a nest of tangled bedclothes, books, magazines, chocolate wrappers and fruit peel.

I noted with annoyance that Sophie was in the act of reading my copy of Anaïs Nin. Anastasia lay next to her, quietly kicking her legs and sucking on her fist. Sophie looked up at me. 'This woman is brilliant,' she said, 'Listen to this.' She read out a rather convoluted passage.

'I hadn't *got* that far yet,' I said grumpily, hoping she would take the hint; but Sophie is always deaf to hints.

She picked herself up from the bed and said casually, 'Can you watch the baby while I have a shower?' She often still called Anastasia 'the baby' as if she didn't yet have a name of her own.

I took Sophie's place on the bed while she pulled her chenille dressing-gown around her, found a towel, and went out. 'Hello, my darling,' I said to Anastasia. 'When are you going to start talking to me?' I liked calling her 'my darling'. It had a formal and old-fashioned ring to it, befitting an aunt. Anastasia moved her lips together in a sucking motion and kicked a little more vigorously. Although she was a long way off talking (she tended to just cry, hiccup, sneeze or burp, and hadn't even given a first smile yet), I always hoped that she might break into conversation at any moment.

I blew a raspberry on her bare tummy and gave her a

finger to hold. I had a wonderful feeling of heightened expectation, which I knew had something to do with the spring day, and a lot to do with having spent almost the entire afternoon with Alex. I am a naturally secretive person, so I hadn't said a word about him to Sophie or Lil. I wanted to keep him to myself; I felt that telling someone would spoil the feeling that I couldn't even explain to myself. But at the same time, I desperately wanted to tell *some*one. I leaned close to Anastasia and whispered, 'I know a boy named Alex!'

Opening Anaïs Nin's *Journals*, I got in some reading while Sophie was gone, with Anastasia holding onto my finger all the while. When Sophie came in from the shower, wearing one of her limp frocks, I said impulsively, 'Why don't you go out for a walk? By yourself . . . I'll take Anastasia.'

'All right,' said Sophie. 'Thanks.' She tidied her hair in front of the mirror, and blew on her glasses and cleaned them. While she was getting ready I put a couple of nappies into a bag and hung it off the handles of the pram, and took it down the steps. Sophie carried Anastasia in her arms. 'She's been fed – shouldn't be hungry for ages,' she said, as she settled her into the pram. Then she kissed her on the cheek, and set off in one direction, while I took Anastasia in the other. We turned and gave each other a final wave, and then I was out alone with my niece for the first time ever.

I stopped for a moment to smile at Anastasia. 'Where will we go, my darling, my dear? We could fly to the moon.'

I was happy and light-headed. Anastasia kicked her legs, and looked at me eagerly. And then she gave me the merest hint of a smile.

I smiled back at her. 'Why, Hetty!' I said. 'You've decided to smile.'

I don't know why I said that. It sounded like someone from the eighteenth or nineteenth century. *'Why, Hetty!'* How ridiculous. But that's what I said, and from that moment on she became known as Hetty.

It was a magical transformation. I had walked up the road with Anastasia in a pram and came back with Hetty. Or rather, I bore her back, triumphantly, the way one bears good tidings. It seemed to be a momentous thing, to have discovered her real name like that, so suddenly and serendipitously, and the pram seemed to be borne on air, as if pulled by angels.

Oscar Wilde knew how important names were in the scheme of things. In his play *The Importance of Being Earnest*, the man who pretended his name was Earnest when he was in the city (though he was called Jack in the country) found out that his name really was Earnest. He had been left in a handbag (a large, capacious handbag) at Victoria Station when he was a baby, and so his entire identity had been muddled.

A perfectly understandable mix-up, and one which we should be thankful hadn't happened to *us* at least, Sophie had told me. And now Anastasia had become Hetty, without even a handbag being implicated. It must have been her true nature asserting itself.

Sophie was already there when we got back. 'Guess what?' I told her. 'I think her name is actually Hetty! And she smiled!'

'She's way too young to smile!' said Sophie. 'It must have been wind.'

'She did smile! I saw it. Oh, I don't care whether you believe me or not. I know what I know. And her name is Hetty, anyway.' I picked Hetty up and danced around the kitchen with her cradled in my arms, moving to invisible joyful music, and smiling into her face.

'You know, I think Hetty was the name I was looking for all along, when I called her Anastasia,' said Sophie.

'That poor child won't know whether she's coming or going!' said Lil. But Hetty knew exactly where she was. She wasn't coming *or* going. She was *here*.

The Red Notebook

Music: 'World Where you live', Crowded House

So. I am reading this book by Sartre. Sar-tra. Sarte. (Say it
soft and in a Frenchy kind of way. How *does* Alex do that
with his mouth?)

Nausea, by Jean-Paul Sartre:

This book is in the form of a diary, written in 1932.
It purports to be written by a man named Antoine
Roquentin, an historian who is living in a small French town
and researching the life of a man in the eighteenth century.

He says that he lives entirely alone, never speaking to
anybody (though this is an exaggeration – he does speak to
all sorts of people). He lives a very odd life. It seems that
he is alienated from himself. He looks on at life as an
observer. He even looks on parts of his own body as if they
were merely an object he was seeing. For instance, he feels
something cold in his hand and notices that he is holding a
doorknob. His thoughts remain misty and nebulous. He
seems to think that human life is meaningless and futile.

It's a very philosophical book. For instance, a man he knows asks him about adventures, and defines an adventure as an event which is out of the ordinary without being necessarily extraordinary. 'People talk of the magic of adventures,' says the man, and asks him if that expression strikes him as accurate. The man asks if *he* has had adventures.

The narrator lies, and tells the man that he has had a few adventures but says to himself that he doesn't even know what the word means any more.

What must it be like, to live in a world where words lose their meaning?

From the dictionary:

adventure, *n*. (the various meanings include:)
    – an undertaking of uncertain outcome; a hazardous enterprise (by this definition life itself is an adventure; so is sitting for the Year 12 exams!)
    – an exciting experience
    – (obsolete) peril, danger
    – to take the chance of, dare
    – to venture
It comes from Middle English *aventure,* from Old French, from Latin *adventura*, meaning 'future'; (a thing) about to happen.

The Yellow Notebook

And very late at night, when she has read enough, she sips absinth in the yellow glow of her reading lamp. The liquid is like a jewel. She sits the glass next to the remaining cube of Turkish delight, and sees the light reflected through them both. The colours remind her of the coloured glass in the old windows of the house she lived in when she was a child.

Outside, the city sleeps. And the fox is out there somewhere, too, somewhere in the wild patch of land that runs from her back garden along to the railway line, and which reminds her of the country, it is so quiet and earthy and secretive.

On one of those misty mornings, when the sunlight falls through fog – still – at nine in the morning, I went to Alex's garage. I knocked, and put my head round the garage door. Alex was lying on top of the bedclothes, spreadeagled naked, asleep.

I rushed outside and stood with the back of my head pressed against the wall, seeing mist fall through the air, seeing beads of water on a spider's web, seeing the blue day stretch up above me, and the grass, plump with green and dew-wet. I could only think of Alex. It wasn't so much seeing him with no clothes on – it was the nakedness of his face as he lay in the abandon of sleep.

I had woken him. I could hear him inside, moving around. Soon he came to the door.

'Hello,' he said. 'I was working late last night and I slept in.'

I looked past him towards the table with the typewriter, wondering whether he meant by *working* that he'd been writing his novel. I expected untidy piles of paper, ashtrays

secret scribbled notebooks 100 secret ser

full of cigarettes and half-empty cups of mint tea. But the typewriter looked as if it had not been touched. It sat mutely on the table with the almost unsullied ream of copy paper beside it.

'I have a job,' he explained. 'A paying one. I pack shelves at one of the supermarkets at night. That's how I pay for food.' He turned to the bench. 'Coffee?' he asked. 'I've decided not to fight my addiction.' He looked wonderfully dishevelled, with stubble on his chin.

He filled the electric kettle, and while it boiled he tipped rather a lot of fresh coffee into a jug, which he then filled with boiling water and allowed to steep with a saucer covering the top of it. Since the first time I'd been there, Alex had acquired a large ceramic jug with a crack near the lip, and another cup.

He started slicing a loaf of heavy wholemeal bread. I sat on his bed, delightfully aware that he had been so recently inhabiting it.

'What is it you want to write about?' I asked.

He looked nervously towards the typewriter, as if it might overhear him, or read his thoughts, or reproach him for lack of activity.

'I don't think I can talk about it,' he said.

'Oh, okay. But why?'

Alex had a coy way of looking at you, and a sly smile that began in his eyes and gradually reached his mouth.

'Because,' he said, and thought a bit more. 'Because I suspect that "works in progress" may sound a bit crazy.'

'Have you been able to write anything?'

'I have. But I threw it away. Sometimes I can only write a few sentences. Sometimes I think that I'll be able to get going with it if I can even get a decent first sentence down on the page.'

'Write the second sentence, then,' I blurted out, and wished I didn't always say the first thing that came into my head.

'Another thing that stops me from writing is that I think that it's probably pointless writing a novel, anyway. I mean, do novels really change the world? So I hover between thinking it's important to write and thinking that the whole thing is a great waste of time.'

Do novels have to change the world? I have to admit that I like novels that appear to be entirely useless, in a world-changing way. I like a novel with lots of people, and conversations, and surprising ways of thinking about things. A novel that you can place against the light and look through, like a piece of pretty glass.

Alex strained the coffee into cups and handed me one. The coffee was dark and strong and bitter, even with the addition of a large amount of sugar. He handed me an ungainly slice of bread, piled high with plum jam, and I ate it.

Alex did not sit on the bed beside me. He had pushed the typewriter over to the edge of the table and sat there with the coffee and a pile of bread and jam in front of him, eating it neatly and without undue haste.

'How's the Sartre going?' he asked. He had to crook his little finger to sip the coffee, his cup was so dainty.

'I'm getting through it. I've got to the part where he starts noticing the existence of things. How they exist so blatantly, somehow. He thinks that nothing matters – it disorients him, rather. In fact, it makes him nauseous.' I looked down at the enormous mug Alex had given me and wondered how on earth I'd be able to finish it. It was a veritable swimming pool of coffee, a lake of coffee.

'If you ask me,' I said, 'I think he was probably a little crazy. If you look at things so closely, you're bound to feel disoriented. Like words. If you say a word over and over it starts to lose all meaning. *Persephone*, for example. *Persephone, Persephone,* what is that? Just a collection of sounds. And *umbrella*. What kind of word is that?'

I looked into the coffee cup and felt a little queasy, as if I might topple into it and drown.

Alex said, 'Don't drink it all if you don't want it. I know what it's like to be overwhelmed by food. My grandparents used to pile up my plate. The table was groaning. I always wished they had a dog that lived under the table that I could slip things to.' He got up and relieved me of my cup. 'Do you want to come for a walk? I like to get the newspaper.'

The town was the same one I'd known my whole life, but there was something about it that day – it was being with Alex – that made it all polished and glowing for me. It was just the usual grid of streets, this one with fig trees all the way along it, this one with a line of bare, hot, front yards without a shrub in sight, with the bright primary colours of children's toys abandoned on paths – I loved it all that day. I felt that the world had opened its arms and clasped me to its bosom.

Alex and I didn't need to say much at all. If I'd been with Sophie we might have played the game where we decided which house we would live in. Sophie always chose something flashy and expensive, but I liked more modest and retiring houses, ones that people wouldn't notice. A small house, suitable for just one family, without any strangers staying overnight in the spare bedrooms. A house where we might have all lived, the four of us, had our parents still been around.

Now, forgetting that Alex and I were not playing the game, I stopped in front of a particular house I liked and said, 'That one! That's where I'd live.' It was a timber cottage, almost entirely overwhelmed by trees, with a wonky verandah and a frog pond in the front garden.

Rather than being surprised by my sudden act of choice, Alex simply smiled and scrutinised the house. 'Yes,' he said, 'I like that one, too. It would be like living in a forest, and when you got bored you could always go out the front and talk to the frogs.'

We bought the newspaper and wandered back, and when we got to the street in front of the lane where he lived, he nodded towards the house next door. 'What do you think that house would be like to live in?' he asked.

It was an old timber house, very nicely kept, with a verandah at the front wrapping round the side. It was all closed up and quiet, and the front door was painted pale blue. There were pink roses growing along the front fence. A frangipani tree in front of the verandah had sprouted its spring leaves, but had not yet flowered.

'I don't know,' I answered. 'I think it would be a quiet life there. A very ordered life.'

Alex had put his arm through mine, very naturally, and he kept hold of it while we made our way round the corner to the laneway. 'My mother used to live there,' he said. 'When she was a girl.'

All I could think was that he was holding my arm.

'I used to visit that house when I was a child. But they're all gone now – my grandparents are dead, and someone else owns it.'

'And your mother?'

'She died when I was nine.'

I was glad that he didn't let go of me, but he said nothing more, and when we reached the door of his garage, I asked, 'Do you feel at home here?'

'I feel at home everywhere,' he said, going inside and throwing the paper down next to all the others on his table. The walls of his garage swallowed these words gratefully.

'Which I suppose is the same as feeling at home nowhere, in the end,' he added.

He looked across at me so frankly, that I felt that in some extraordinary way he was only one atom separated from myself. And yet, we still knew hardly anything about each other.

'My father and I,' he said, 'We were so sad when she died. But we kept it inside ourselves. He never really allowed us to grieve. We got on with our lives.'

I didn't know what to say. I had no experience of death. I had no experience of mothers. He looked so dreadfully sad though, and I knew what that felt like. In my more dramatic moments I felt that I had been sad my whole life. Was that what drew me to Alex, then? Sadness calling to sadness?

He made us more coffee, and divvied up the newspaper so we could read some each. We sat out at a table under a frangipani tree and read and sipped coffee.

'I know nothing about you, Kate,' he said. 'Tell me something about you. The first thing that comes into your head.' He said it softly and casually, but in a way that implied that he really wanted to know. I felt startled. Alex was a dangerous person, asking questions like that. What if I started telling him? I couldn't; I was so used to keeping things to myself.

'I'm an aunt,' I said. My voice sounded surprised, and I was surprised. I had no idea that would pop out.

'An aunt. Really?'

'Yes. My sister has a baby. A girl, she's only a few weeks old. Her name's Hetty. It used to be Anastasia . . .'

'Ah, Anastasia. A Russian name.'

'Yes, but it turned out that her name was Hetty all along.'

Alex nodded.

'I love her,' I said. 'And – that's it really.' I went back to reading my newspaper, and when I caught him looking at me, he turned away.

The Red Notebook

Living in this place is enough to drive you batty. For a start, there are almost always people here. Strangers. Strange strangers. All right, I know it's a guest house and it's our living but . . .

Here is an example of the type of people we attract. One man didn't come out of his room for an entire week (not even to go to the toilet, as far as we knew), and Lil thought he might be dead (of course he wasn't). So now, whenever we don't see a guest for a while, Sophie always says dramatically, 'They must be dead!' to rile Lil. It turned out he'd been peeing out the window (we found the evidence on the windowsill – what else he'd done out there we don't like to imagine!). And he left behind a huge pile of chip packets and chocolate wrappers and empty bottles of Coke, so he'd obviously come prepared to seclude himself.

The guests always expect things to be perfect too, which is annoying, when it's so cheap. What do they expect? Frogs in the toilet is a frequent complaint (as if we're going to go plunging our hands into the bowl to get them out!). And they don't like the carpet snake that lives in the rafters of the verandah sometimes. Well, hello! This is the north coast! The carpet snakes were here before we were! (Lil says I should refrain from telling them we like the snakes because they catch the rats. We don't mention the R word around here.)

We rarely eat a meal without a guest wanting something. And because The Customer Is Always Right, we have to be polite all the time.

The things the guests leave behind tells you what they're like (this is just a partial list):

about twenty copies of Stephen King novels, dog-eared to various degrees, which Lil put in the bookshelves in the common lounge

and eight copies of *A Year in Tuscany*, at last count

Someone left *On The Road* by Jack Kerouac, which Sophie snaffled but to my knowledge has never read – it lies in one of the piles in her room

Also *The Joy of Sex*, much thumbed, which Lil threw in the bin with an expression on her face as if she'd just sucked a lemon (though it was retrieved by Sophie, who later tossed it out again).

And various personal items, including too many extremely ragged toothbrushes and almost-empty packets of Disprin to mention, an old leather motorbike jacket with zip-up pockets and a bright red lipstick (worn down to the base) in the pocket. There was a belt made of old Chinese coins, very beautiful, held in case the owner returned, three pairs of ear-rings and two single ones, an unopened packet of condoms (Savage Pleasure brand), a total of ten pots of Tiger Balm, a pair of cowboy boots worn down at the sides, a diary (which Lil wouldn't allow us to read, but which was also held in case the owner returned), and a love letter, which we did read, from someone called Tom, to Theo. It was still connected to its writing pad, and full of unrequited longing. It confirmed me in my determination never to fall in love.

When I arrived back from visiting Alex that day, there was no one at home. Two people had booked in earlier, but had probably gone out again, and so had Lil. Sophie and Hetty weren't there either. There was a note from Lil on the front door saying, *Gone shopping etc. Back soon*.

Houses without people in them have a particular feel. It is as though you have caught them in the act of being entirely themselves. They resist re-entry, insisting on retaining an uninhabited atmosphere, so that you feel you need to creep about. Only gradually will they begin to warm to you again.

I listened to my own footsteps sounding down the hallway, hollow and questioning. In the kitchen I found the remains of an apple teacake, which I scoffed standing at the sink in order to catch any crumbs, washing it down with orange juice and staring out through the panes of coloured glass.

I went on a tour of the house. Sophie's room was awash

with books and baby's clothes. *Anaïs Nin* was splayed on the floor next to the bed, the author gazing towards the ceiling.

Lil's room was neater, her bed made, with a bed doll in a garish mauve and silver crinoline dress sitting at its centre. I once adored this doll; its hair was all frizzy from when I used to comb it.

On the bedside table were two photograph frames. One held two pictures of Lil's son, Alan. In one he was a small boy with slicked-back hair and neatly pressed shorts and shirt, with a tie. In the other he was a young man with long shining hair and a beard, wearing jeans and a hippy shirt. In both he smiled confidently into the camera as if he loved himself and the whole world.

The other frame contained a picture of me and Sophie together, when I was about five and Sophie eight. We were dressed in beautiful little frocks (how Lil had loved dressing us up! Now she always grumbled that neither of us had any regard for our looks. 'Girls these days just have no idea,' she said, 'of how to dress nicely.')

I flopped onto my back on Lil's bed and picked up the doll. It was a difficult doll to hug, with a prickly skirt that warded you off. I lay there and thought about my visit to Alex. His mother had died, and now he lived next door to her childhood home in an old garage. Is that why he had come to this place? To be close to the house where his mother had grown up?

I seldom admitted it to myself, but I did feel an intense curiosity at times about my own mother. This Margaret Thomas, with the ordinary name and the wild reputation among the daughters who barely knew her. How could she leave us like that? Why would she do it? I thought of Sophie's description of the dark, gypsy-like woman wearing the red dress. Were children too constricting to her? Did she go off in search of adventure? Was that what she wanted? A life without the constraints of *us*?

Unlike Alex, I wouldn't know where to even begin looking for memories of my mother.

I tossed the doll back onto the bed and got to my feet. Opening the drawer of the dressing-table, I looked at the cosmetics that Lil kept tumbled inside it – face powder and something she called 'rouge', though it was really blusher, and endless lipsticks, many of which had worn right down. It seemed that Lil threw nothing out. When she died, Sophie and I would have to spend years clearing out her things.

When she died. There had been times in her life when I'd feared Lil's death, and thought that it was imminent, but now I couldn't believe that she would ever die. She was like one of those everlasting daisies, all dried out and crinkly even while they were alive. She'd last forever.

I took the lid off one of the lipsticks and shaded in my mouth, staring at my reflection in the mirror. The bright red was startling against my white skin; I looked like a vampire after a recent meal. I found a black eyebrow pencil and licked the tip of it, then used it to make a dark spot on my cheek, near my mouth – what Lil called a *beauty spot*, though what was beautiful about it I couldn't imagine. It was some old-fashioned thing that women did, apparently – perhaps the hideousness of the mark made the rest of you look quite beautiful in contrast.

Going to the wardrobe, I opened it and ran my hands through Lil's dresses. They had the smell of a second-hand clothes shop; the scent of fabric had been overwhelmed by the faint rancid odour of people, which couldn't be erased from even the cleanest clothes.

We used to love going through Lil's wardrobe on dull afternoons, and Lil had never minded. I knew every dress by heart – the glittery blackish-silver sheath that Lil wore to the funerals of her friends, the one with the red roses and gathered skirt, the white jersey with the cowl neck, the plain shift with Pop Art patterns on it, the red dress with bat-wing sleeves . . . Lil had owned these dresses for hundreds of years and it was almost a library of every dress style that had ever existed.

At the very end of the row was the Man's Suit. Sophie and I used to speculate about the suit. (Had it belonged to a lover of Lil, or to our father? Or had a guest simply forgotten it, and Lil kept it in case they returned?) We'd learned, when Lil overheard us discussing it, that it had belonged to her son Alan. Lil told us that she couldn't bear to throw it out after he died. And then her face had closed up. She hadn't wanted to talk about it.

Lil had so much stuff that if she did die (when she died . . .), there'd be no shortage of mementoes to remember her by. Whereas, of our own mother we had nothing: not a photograph, or a bracelet, or even one single worn-down lipstick.

When I was seven, I had walked home from school for the first time on my own.

This was an important milestone, for Lil had expressly forbidden me to do it. Sophie was meant to walk me to and from school each day.

Sophie hated having to do this – it stopped her running off immediately with her friends and doing whatever important things she was doing in those days. On this particular day, she said, 'Kate. I have to go to Jane's house *right now* – I don't have time to take you home first. You can walk by yourself, can't you? *But don't tell Lil.* Tell her I saw you to the door first.'

I set off. The lollipop man helped us all cross the road near the school, and I had no other busy crossing to contend with after that. I ignored the boys on the corner who always teased me, and said *pooh!* to the black dog that lived behind a high timber fence, and it lunged towards me, barking, making the fence shudder with its weight. I took an apple from my bag to feed the goat with the hard demonic eyes that lived tethered on the empty block three houses from Samarkand. I was as good as home at that point, and as the goat took the fruit from my hand I savoured the feeling of having achieved something that I had been absolutely forbidden to do.

That walk had been a cinch, really, and I felt invincible. I was purple with importance by the time I reached Samarkand. I paused at the bottom of the steps that seemed to weave their way forever up the front, took a deep breath and toiled up them, knocking my school case against each step as I ascended.

The house was silent. There seemed to be no one there. This was unusual, because Lil was always there when we got home. It was usual for several of the guests to be milling about on the verandah or in the lounge room as well.

The kitchen was empty, so I went looking for Lil in all the usual places. She wasn't in the television room, and she wasn't hiding with a book on the overstuffed sofa on the verandah. The next most likely place for her to be was in her room, and that was dead silent. I crept to the doorway.

Lil's room was in darkness; the curtains drawn. I went up to the bed: Lil lay so still that I knew she was dead. Whatever had made her Lil had departed. The room had a feeling of absence in it. I pulled a chair over next to the bed and sat with her, not touching her, just gazing at her face in the faint light that came through the window. Lil kept a tin of lemon sweets on her bedside table. I reached over and removed one from its bed of powdered sugar, and sucked slowly on it, allowing it to dissolve on my tongue.

What would happen to us now that Lil was gone? Who would look after us? I missed Lil already. A hole had opened up inside me, but no tears came.

If one did creep in a ticklish track down my cheek, I just licked it away. Having finished the lemon sweet, I reached for the tin and sat with it opened on my lap, with my head bowed. I took another sweet and crunched savagely into it.

When I looked up, Lil's eyes had opened, and she was looking at me, though no other part of her had moved. It was like being observed by a statue.

'Did you ask if you could have those, madam?'

I dropped the tin at once, and sweets rattled onto the floor.

I had tasted grief. It would always taste of sugary lemon. It would feel like the shard of a hard sweet against my tongue; a film of sugar across my teeth.

I took the *Anaïs Nin* (*my* Anaïs Nin) from Sophie's room, and lay on my back on the verandah floor, just near the front door, where I could read by the low rays of the sun that came slanting through the trees. I looked up at the pattern of the galvanised iron, and the old timber rafters, and imagined the house spinning about me – the rafters, the tin roof and the draughty timber walls, the gappy floorboards, and the doors and windows that let in all the light and sound from the world outside. The house was at once substantial and insubstantial; I thought that if it could spin fast enough, then it would all come apart and circle and circle me, and then just as easily settle into place again, every nail and board and bit of tin. I might be leaving soon, but I knew that for as long as I lived I would dream of Samarkand; in my sleep I would enter its walls and tread its worn floors, and wake filled with peace and foreboding. Samarkand was as much a part of me as my skin.

The Yellow Notebook

Some nights, when she gets home from work, she can't bear to cook, and she needs something more than solitude. So she takes a book and goes out to a cafe she knows, and where they know her. She orders her usual, a plate of spaghetti with mussels, a green salad, and a glass of red wine, and eats slowly, watching the people walk by in the street, and the lights of passing cars. She knows better than to eat and read at the same time. She did that when she was young, but it means you can't enjoy either experience to the full. So it is only when she is replete that she pushes her plate aside and begins to read.

The cafe is full of people and their talk washes over her. She is unselfconscious, eating out on her own, and doesn't notice that people look at her, and wonder about who she might be, so lovely and all alone.

She becomes aware of someone standing near her table – she looks up, and sees a man, tall and slender, with a slim brown face and watchful, friendly eyes. 'May I sit with you?' he asks. She assents with an inclination of her head.

'I've noticed you here before,' he says, as he sits down. There is nothing sleazy or pushy about him. 'My name's Alexander,' he says. 'What's yours?'

'Katerina,' she says, closing her book and glancing at him across the table.

'I'm sorry I interrupted. But I could see you reading one of my favourite books –'

'Sartre?' she says.

He nods. 'Yes, Sartre . . .'

When Lil and Sophie arrived home that afternoon, I was still lying on the floor of the verandah, reading.

'Move that body of yours please, madam. My old legs can't step over you!' Lil was accompanied by fistfuls of plastic bags which the taxi driver deposited at the top of the stairs, and which I helped her haul in to dump on the kitchen table. Sophie snatched *The Journals of Anaïs Nin* from my hand and disappeared with Hetty to her room.

'Been into my make-up again?' said Lil comfortably, putting on the kettle for a cup of tea.

I poked around in the contents of the bags, looking for something interesting to eat. I found a packet of biscuits and opened it. 'I've *told* you we shouldn't use plastic bags!' I said, with my mouth full, as Lil emptied the bags and they mounted in a flimsy pile on the table. 'You should get those calico ones they sell. These will all end up in some landfill or dumped into the sea, and turtles will eat them thinking they're jellyfish! Did you know they found a whale with about a tonne of this stuff in its gut?'

'Some days,' said Lil, 'there are more important things to think about than remembering to buy a whole lot of calico bags. We've just spent most of the afternoon down at the Social, sorting out Sophie's payments.' She shovelled four cartons of eggs into the fridge, along with two bulk packs of bacon and several pounds of butter, like someone stoking the boiler on an old steam train.

'It's called Centrelink now,' I told her, arranging fruit in a bowl with a great deal of finesse. I put the yellow lemons with some golden pears, and put green apples into a bowl with a red capsicum on top.

'Very nice, I'm sure,' commented Lil sourly, stopping for a moment and surveying the fruit with one hand on her hip, before turning round to stack loaves of bread onto a corner of the bench.

Sophie drifted in and casually plucked an apple from the bowl, biting into it dreamily.

'Well,' said Lil, 'now you know,' obviously referring to something which I had not been party to. 'That will be your life for the next twenty years or so, unless you stir your stumps and support yourself and that baby with your own hands, the way I did. You won't get much joy from them, nor money either. Waiting and explaining, that will about be the size of it. Handing them bits of paper till they're coming out your ears.'

'Just leave me!' said Sophie. 'I'm too tired to think about it now. Or talk. Or have you going on at me.'

'How can she hand them bits of paper till they're coming out her ears?' I said, but they ignored me.

'I *will* do something,' said Sophie. 'Just, not yet. She's only a couple of months old. Even working women have at least a couple of months off when they have a baby!'

'Just so long as you're thinking about it,' said Lil, nodding. 'You can't simply let your life . . . drift.' She gestured with her hands as though a boat was teetering on the seas.

'Oh, so running a *really classy* guest house is doing something with your life!' retorted Sophie.

'It kept me and my boy,' said Lil, quietly, with her back to us, making the tea. 'It kept you.'

I ran out and up to Sophie's room where Hetty lay in her crib. 'Everyone's so *edgy*,' I whispered to her. 'Can I come and play with you?'

I took Hetty onto the bed with me and kissed her on the cheek, where my lips left a red smudge. I wiped it away with some spit on a corner of a sheet, then rescued Anaïs from under Sophie's pillow and resumed reading where I'd left off. *Anaïs's mother is very old. Every time she visits her she feels it might be for the last time. She says that she was always preparing herself for the separation, and would have liked to be able to sense when she should be there.*

It was true, I thought, the people we love might be gone at any time. And yet Anaïs Nin's relationship with her mother was rather edgy. Isn't that always the way? We love people, and yet . . .

'Lil wants you to help with the dinner,' said Sophie, coming into the room. 'She's that done in, she says, and implies it's all my fault.'

I relinquished the book again (*my* book – I'd found it in the bookshop, and I was sure I needed it far more than

Sophie did). To compensate, I snatched up the copy of *A Room of One's Own* that I'd bought for Sophie all that time ago – I'm sure Sophie had never even looked at it – and took myself to the kitchen.

A chicken, as pale as lard, sat trussed on a plate in the middle of the table. 'Sophie won't eat that,' I said. 'You'll have to open some nutmeat.'

'It's white meat,' said Lil. 'That's as good as a vegetable, in my books.'

'Chooks still have red blood,' I told her. 'They have mothers. Isn't that a definition of an animal?'

I peeled the potatoes that Lil thrust at me, and topped and tailed the beans. *If I do brilliantly in these exams,* I thought, *it will be a miracle. And I'm up against all these people who go to private schools, whose parents are lawyers and everything, and those parents are* even now *cooking them something really nutritious and good for their brains – something like deep-sea fish with a sunflower sprout salad, washed down with a shot of wheat-grass juice.*

While the dinner was cooking, I brought all my stuff down to the kitchen to study. It made an impressive array on the kitchen table – sheets of businesslike diagrams, lined cards scrawled with notes in different-coloured ink, notebooks crammed with summaries, and textbooks decorated with highlighted underlinings. It made me look like a serious student.

Working in the kitchen reminded me of when I was little, and did my homework there, with Lil pottering about taking the lid off one pot and popping a lid on another.

This kitchen was the only one that I had ever known. When we had arrived at Samarkand I was only as tall as the table. I used to creep around under it. It was a different world down there, my own world. Lil had a cat in those days, a striped, slender creature with a bung eye. There had been two bowls in the corner of the room for it, one for meat and one for milk.

The floor covering had been renewed since then. I remember the red-and- black pattern of the old lino. It was black and sticky where it had worn through, as rough as a kitten's tongue. From under the table you could see only legs, and things that had found their way there: stray peas, and dead moths, and a trail of ants to the cat bowls. 'What are you up to down there?' Lil would ask. 'Come up here to me.' She'd held out her arms.

I'd spent most of my time in the kitchen with Lil, who handed me a never-ending stream of food. I ate it all gratefully: bread with Vegemite, Saos with tomatoes and cheese, slices of apple cake. 'You've got hollow legs!'

The rest of the house had been wonderful and mysterious. There were rooms and rooms: rooms that I wasn't allowed into, that belonged to the guests ('Hello. Who do *you* belong to?' I didn't belong to anyone. If anything, I belonged to the house), and narrow rooms that could be hidden in, among brooms and buckets and shelves full of sheets, still smelling of the sun. There were verandahs, two levels of them, scattered with collapsing chairs and sofas, open to the sky, or shaded by a tangle of trees with red spikes of sunlight shafting through them. Leaves blew onto the verandah and sat in drifts on the floor.

Now, here I was, only months from possibly leaving the place altogether, and I didn't even know exactly how I felt about it, only that the thought sometimes made me miserable, and sometimes exhilarated, and sometimes extremely scared. I felt guilty, too, because I'd put in my choices for university, and hadn't told Lil or Sophie what they were. They assumed I would go to university in Lismore, but I had applied for a university in Sydney as my first choice. I didn't know when I'd get up enough courage to tell them this.

'You always have been one for spreading yourself,' Lil grumbled, taking the chook from the oven and heaving it onto the table with a bump. Fat splashed all over my carefully arranged notes. I wiped it off with a tea towel.

'If you will put your things everywhere . . .'

I don't know why I snapped at her the way I did. I said, 'Well, I'll be leaving soon, and then I won't annoy you!'

Lil turned the potatoes and put the chook back into the oven without a word, and I slowly packed away my books. I took my things to my room, where I immediately burst into tears.

The truth was, I felt less sure about heading off to live in a city than I made out to myself. Cities were unfamiliar to me. We went to the Gold Coast sometimes, but that wasn't a real city, just an endless strip of high-rise buildings running between the mountains and the sea. We went to Brisbane – only a couple of hours away on the bus – to shop occasionally, but I had only been to Sydney once, as far as I could remember.

Lil couldn't get away from Samarkand often, that was the problem, so we'd had very few holidays. The one time we went to Sydney, when I was ten, Lil called a 'busman's holiday', because she had swapped places with a friend of hers who ran a bed and breakfast in Sydney.

The place in Sydney was a much posher establishment than Samarkand was, and the people expected a higher level of service. It was a big old house close to the city (called, rather grandly, 'the Mansions'), with a pretty back garden and polished floors, and nicer rooms, with good bedspreads and flowers and ensuite bathrooms. The breakfasts couldn't be just slapped down on tables any old how, and there was a need to be charming to the guests. When Lil got back home to Samarkand she said it was a blessed relief. She never changed places with her friend again.

But the trip to Sydney had a magical charm for me. I loved the idea of all that life throbbing away out there, not far from where we slept. And that life could be stepped out into at any time. Not far from the Mansions there were busy shopping streets. I found shops filled with books, and I loitered in them reading for as long as I decently could. I bought books with whatever money Lil gave to me. That was when I'd bought my copy of *Great Expectations*. It was so pleasingly packed with words, and it looked so grown-up – I kept it for a couple of years as a kind of talisman before I finally got around to reading it. It had promised much, and it didn't disappoint me. It was so full of images of darkness and light, and I saw something of myself in Pip, the boy who wanted to escape his humble origins. It was a book that grew with me, so that each time I read it there was something more, something I'd been blind to at an earlier reading. It was a book I felt I could live with my whole life.

I also discovered Turkish delight. It winked at me from the window of a shop, and I bought two pieces (it was terrifyingly more expensive than chocolate), and took it home to share with Sophie.

It tasted like a rosebud exploding on my tongue, and was as sweet and sticky as soft toffee. I lay on the bed and almost passed out in a sensation of rose-flavoured pink, and when I recovered I sat up and declared, 'I'm going to come and live in this city when I grow up and eat *nothing* but Turkish delight!'

'Would you leave me, Katie?' asked Lil, liltingly, shooing me off the bed so I didn't muck up the clean cover.

'I would,' I told her, callously. 'Yes, I would.'

I don't know why Lil insisted that we eat together at the table every night, because Sophie usually sat there with a book, and tonight, because I felt sad and confused after my kind-of altercation with Lil, I did too. I started on the book by Virginia Woolf, *A Room of One's Own*, which began by describing two dinners that Woolf went to in the early 1920s, first at a men's college at a university, and then at a women's college. The men were given infinitely better food, and they had wine as well. Virginia Woolf came to the conclusion that 'One cannot think well, love well, sleep well, if one has not dined well . . . A good dinner is of great importance to good talk.'

There was very little talk at our table that night. Far from not wanting to eat meat, Sophie distinguished herself by eating chook and only chook – she wanted no potatoes, peas or pumpkin. She pulled the flesh apart slowly, and ate with her fingers while Hetty stayed clamped to her breast. She looked up from *The Journals of Anaïs Nin* only to tear another piece from the carcass on the platter in front of her. Lil consumed the parson's nose with an air of affronted dignity, deliberately not looking at either of us. Lil considered the parson's nose a delicacy, though it was just pure fat and technically the chook's bum, but she didn't appear to be particularly enjoying it that night. It was a mournful meal, and I thought that Virginia Woolf should have added that one could not dine well unless there was good talk as well.

At least there was always Hetty. After the washing-up was done, I ran to see her, and lay on Sophie's bed watching her sleep. She was the sort of baby you *could* watch sleep. Her face had an ever-changing array of expressions and every one of them was adorable. She changed her appearance with regularity as well, as though trying out all her options. At that time it seemed that she was going for the bald look. She must have determined to lose her amazing crop of dark hair, and all her body hair as well. She had done it by stealth, for it seemed to have happened gradually. Without our knowing it, she metamorphosed into a bald baby. We woke up one day and said, 'Hello, where's all Hetty's hair gone?'

I said impulsively, to Sophie, 'Why don't you go out? You never do. I could look after Hetty.'

Sophie looked up with a puzzled expression. 'Where would I want to go?' she said.

'Oh, you know – all the places you used to go. Round to Carmen or Rafaella's. Or to the pub to hear some music. Just for a walk, if you wanted to. If you like I could have her in my room all night, and you could just get a whole night's sleep for once.'

'What about when she gets hungry?'

'Express some milk.'

'Takes too long.'

'Well, just go out for a little while then. When she wakes up I'll bring her round for a feed.'

I watched Sophie get ready. This involved very little, even for her. She cleaned her glasses and stuck them back onto her face, and she brushed her hair and straightened up her dress in front of the mirror. 'I look dowdy, don't I?' she said, sadly.

'You could put a clean dress on.'

'You're saying this one's dirty.'

'No! It's just looking a bit . . . slept-in.'

Sophie unbuttoned her dress, let it fall to her feet and kicked it away. She picked up another from the floor, sniffed it, and put it on, smoothing out the creases over her hips. 'Anyway,' she said steadily, looking at herself in the mirror, 'What would I want to dress up *for*?'

When she'd gone, I took the sleeping Hetty around to my room. Now that I didn't have to get up for school I had allowed my night-owl tendencies to take over. These days, I stayed up almost all night studying, and got up late, even napping sometimes in the afternoons. I liked it at night when everyone was asleep, and the light shone out hopefully in my little room at the back of the house like a remote outpost in a jungle.

That night, while Hetty slept, I sat at my desk where the lamp made a circle of light in the dark room. I felt already stale with all the things I was meant to be studying. I had read every one of the books for English too many times already, so I did a few Maths problems. Then I picked up the book I'd begun reading that night in the kitchen and started on it again.

Hetty made a lot of noise while she slept. She was like a

snorting little animal; once, she opened her eyes and murmured. I leaned over her and listened, thinking that she might say something intelligible, but it was just sounds.

After midnight I went to the kitchen to make a cup of hot chocolate, and on the way back I passed the TV room, where there was just the flickering light of the television in the darkened room. Lil was there alone, sitting in an armchair, a giant-sized block of chocolate on her lap, her face illuminated by the light from the television. She was watching an old black-and-white movie, and she was in tears. Crying over a movie wasn't unusual for her, but I couldn't help feeling that she was crying over something else.

Lil's eyes made a slight movement in my direction when I appeared at the doorway, but she kept her face firmly in the direction of the television. It was as if she couldn't look at me, and I hurried away, back to the solace of my room and Hetty. I knew that I'd upset her with my thoughtless threat of leaving, but I didn't know how to apologise – didn't know if I *wanted* to apologise – at that moment.

Hetty breathed as peacefully as a drowsing cat, her mouth a fat cupid's bow. Her eyes fluttered open, then she was asleep again. I watched her; she was so new and unworn, her feet so soft and untrod upon the ground.

I tried to forget about Lil, and read with one hand on Hetty's cradle. Virginia Woolf urged young women to drink wine and have a room of their own. 'So long as you write what you wish to write, that is all that matters; and whether it matters for ages or only for hours, nobody can say.'

I thought of Alex, who said he couldn't even make a start. He couldn't make his words matter to himself, even for a little while.

I scribbled in my Red Notebook, writing about my guilt when I'd seen Lil in tears. I wrote out some quotations from Virginia Woolf. Then I went onto the verandah and sat on the sofa and looked out into the trees. The smell of their dank vegetation was in the night air. There were secretive rustlings along the branches which Sophie and I always said were possums, while Lil always swore they were rats. Sophie always retorted that she had absolutely no romantic imagination; Lil always said that we had too much.

Some people walked along the back lane; a child said plaintively, 'Mu-um . . .' A dog howled somewhere. I heard Sophie come home; she didn't come round to my room to check on Hetty so I assumed she had gone to bed. I imagined that Lil had, as well. The house was silent, and I sat there for a long while.

Hetty began to cry, so I changed her nappy and lifted her from her cradle with soft words of love to soothe her, then wrapped her in a blanket and took her around the verandah to Sophie's room. I switched on Sophie's reading light and shook her awake, helped Hetty find a breast, and watched her feed. She was such a greedy baby! She drank until she was full, gave a drunken smile, and closed her eyes. I lifted her up and took her back to my room and put her to bed.

I dreamed I was in the middle of an exam, and Virginia Woolf was urging me to write! To write whatever I wanted to. But somewhere there was a baby crying, and I apologised to Virginia Woolf and went to comfort it.

I was woken by Hetty screaming. It was eight in the morning, and she was wet and starving hungry again.

The Red Notebook

Spring. Flowers bursting out everywhere.

A List:

> Lil – an enormous red, overblown rose, petals dropping onto the table.
> Sophie – a very new rose, hardly unfolded, but with lots of potential to go the way that Lil has.
> Hetty – something very small and neat and perfect – a chamomile flower.
> Marjorie – a pansy, all velvety and beautiful.
> me – ????

It was spring. I had that to be thankful for, even if the exams were looming ever closer. I had no time to visit Alex, and spent as long with my books as I could stand, glad on Saturdays when I could go to work at the cafe and escape it all.

I worked with a girl called Hannah, with breasts that peeped over the top of her blouse. I tried not to look, but often found myself stealing glimpses of them. Hannah and I worked very companionably, and never got in each other's way. As the morning wore on towards lunchtime and the cafe became even busier, it became a kind of dance behind the crowded counter, with our hips and arms always miraculously gliding past each other. By the time the cafe emptied out again, I was moist with sweat.

Hannah brought me a freshly squeezed juice, all frothy on the top, which I sipped in the back yard with the scent of jasmine from the side fence making me almost faint with delight. I wondered why on earth I wanted to go to university when it was so enjoyable simply working in a cafe.

Hannah was a little older than me, and had left school in Year 10. She seemed such a blithe, uncomplicated girl. If she was a flower she would be a gardenia, full and white and sweet-scented.

(Because of Oscar Wilde, I sometimes wondered what kind of flower certain people would be. I had seen a photo of Virginia Woolf taken a hundred years ago when she was my age, and she was simply beautiful, a violet, with a graceful bowed neck and a delicate face. If Alex was a flower, what would he be? Something that dwelt in the shaded, damp, secretive part of the garden. Something darkly purplish.)

Hannah and I closed up the shop and mopped out the kitchen, and then this gardenia of a girl asked me if I wanted to come round to her place.

She lived just a block away from the cafe in a share house, a lopsided timber place with rattly front steps and a back yard which contained nothing but a clothesline and a frangipani tree with creamy flowers. Hannah made jasmine tea, which we sipped on the back steps. She had a black cat named Blanche that wove between our legs as we talked. One of her flatmates, a girl named Clive, had the thinnest legs I had ever seen, and was doing a load of washing in an old machine that sat under the house. She pegged the clothes out on the rusty Hill's Hoist, and I was utterly happy at that moment, sitting on the back step watching the bright clothes go up onto the line with the blue sky above.

I liked Hannah because she was calm and unassuming. I liked her speed and efficiency with a mop, her encompassing smile, and the little mole at the side of her face, so darkly beautiful on her white skin. She was a different style of girl from Marjorie, who could be nervy and preoccupied. With

Hannah, I could be a different person. With Hannah, I was Kate the weary waitress, rather than Kate the ambitious student. Life was not more complicated than the next vegetarian focaccia and soya-milk latte.

And yet I found out that Hannah was not content with her life. 'I swore when I left school that I would never work as a waitress and I would never work weekends, and here I am doing both,' she said, tipping her remaining tea out over the edge of the steps.

'What would you like to do?'

'Design dresses. I'd like to do a TAFE fashion course or something. Move to Sydney – the best course is down there. Come on, I'll show you what I do.'

We went to her room. Hannah had more clothes than anyone could possibly know what to do with. They hung from the picture rail, overlapping each other, all around the room, and on a makeshift rack in the corner. They were mostly old clothes from op shops, many of which she'd remodelled, sometimes pulling them apart completely and re-using the fabric. She'd made an old chenille dressing-gown into a mini-skirt, and a kimono into several blouses.

'Try something on,' she urged, 'and if you like it, I'll give it to you.'

'I'm not really . . . a clothes sort of person,' I told her.

'Oh, come on. My clothes would look so good on you. You've got a great body. Now, let me see . . .' She went through the rack and pulled one out. She threw it at me, and I caught it. 'Try that.'

It was a red dress made of some sort of stretchy fabric, with long sleeves and a low, scooped neck. Shyly, I changed into it, turning round to look at myself in the mirror. I liked what I saw. It came to just above my knees and hugged my body.

'It fits so well I must have made it for you,' said Hannah. 'You've got to keep it.'

'Oh, no . . .' I looked at myself in the mirror with alarm. 'I couldn't . . .'

'Look that sexy?'

'Do I?'

'You could have adventures in that dress,' said Hannah, chuckling.

'Adventures?'

'Yep. Definitely.'

'What sort of adventures, exactly? Or even approximately.'

'Any kind you like. Wear it home today. Oh go on, Kate. It's no big deal. The fabric cost me next to nothing.'

'All right. Thank you.'

I kept the red dress on, and put my old clothes into a plastic bag. On the table beside the bed I noticed a framed photograph of a young man. 'Your boyfriend?' I asked.

Hannah laid the picture face down on the table. 'Used to be,' she said, and turned her face away. 'I can't get rid of it. I still love him.'

I wondered how I could have ever imagined Hannah to be uncomplicated. How I could have read as many books as I had and still imagined that there was one single completely blithe person upon this earth. There were people everywhere who had an appearance of absolute normality, but who carried a weight of hurt and sorrow inside them. You could never assume anything about people.

In Hannah's red dress, I found myself not walking directly home afterwards, but making my way to Alex's place. It wasn't a conscious decision, I just went, but at the same time, I knew where I was going.

Alex wasn't there, but that didn't matter. He might have been absent, but the place was full of him. It was full of him in its sparse, neat, orderly way. His bed with the blanket tucked tightly over it. His two cups and a teaspoon with a Chinese man on the handle that he'd found one day in the street. His washing-up bowl turned upside down with a sponge beside it.

The typewriter sat silently on the table. Next to it was the pile of newspapers that he seemed to collect and never throw out. FREE THE REFUGEES said the newspaper on the top of the pile, the one he'd bought from the boy in the street that day. I wished in a vague way that I could share his intense interest in news and politics, but in my heart I was happy in the world of books written by people a long time ago.

I sat down in the middle of the floor. The place was still, and silent. I was surprised to find that I wasn't actually waiting for Alex; I was simply being in the place where he'd been. I'd have been mortified if he'd arrived and found me there, dressed in the red dress that you could have adventures in.

There was a new object in Alex's space, a small battered suitcase with a yellow plaid design, sitting on the end of the bench. I stood up, and feeling like an intruder for the first time, went across and clicked the rusty locks open. They sprang back with a force that surprised me. The suitcase was empty.

Inside the lid was a sticker saying that it had been made by the Globite company. The name PJ O'TOOLE was written in block letters under that, now faded and worn. On the front, just under the handle, the same hand had written the words WINTER STUFF.

When I got back home, I went straight to Sophie's room, pushing my way through the flimsy curtains that drifted across her doorway to the verandah. Sophie was lying on one elbow, with Hetty beside her. She turned to face me as I came in. She'd been crying.

Sophie hardly ever cried. I thought at first that she must have been reading *Anna Karenina* again. The part where Anna walks under the train and kills herself always devastated Sophie.

She wiped her face and said savagely, 'Well? What do you want?'

I stood awkwardly, marooned in the middle of the floor. 'What's the matter?' I asked with dismay. I could see that something more than Anna Karenina was upsetting her.

'Nothing.'

Hetty turned her head to the sound of her mother's voice.

I dropped to my knees onto the bed and said, 'It must be something.' Sophie made no reply, and did not look at me.

'Don't be sad,' I said. 'Look at Hetty. She's beautiful. How can you be sad when you have her?'

'It's not the same,' said Sophie. Her voice was muffled.

I knelt there, not understanding.

'Hetty's not enough for me. I want Marcus, you idiot.'

The Red Notebook

I am sitting on a chair with my legs on the verandah rail. Sophie is swinging Hetty in the hammock. Hetty is stark naked, and Sophie is in an old bikini that barely covers her breasts, and shows her stomach, patterned with silvery stretch marks. The marks remind me of a shoal of small fish, the kind that turn with one accord in a flash of silver.

Sophie kisses Hetty tenderly on each cheek. Then she turns her over and lowers her gently onto her belly, so that they are lying front to front. She strokes Hetty's back, and the two of them close their eyes, basking in the sun like seals.

How vulnerable people are. How tiny and helpless a baby is. Hetty's head is as bald as an egg, and as strong, and tender and fragile too. Her limbs are still so unco-ordinated, her neck a wavery stalk.

I think about what Sophie told me yesterday about Marcus. There is a lot about her relationship with him I don't know. Did she get pregnant on purpose because she knew he would leave soon and she wanted to keep a part of him? Or was she just careless? Did she want sex because that is the closest you can get to someone, and she needs that?

I remember that when we first came here, we craved for Lil to touch us. I remember always holding her hand, and hugging her. I wouldn't let her go. People like us – like me and Sophie – need to be very careful of people. Because we are in danger of doing anything for them, anything for affection.

Now Sophie has gone, and the hammock is hanging empty. It still sways from her being there. It is like having an invisible sister rocking back and forth in front of me.

On **this particular day** I had swept
the verandahs and hung out my sheets to flap in the breeze.
Hetty lay in her basket beside me with her nappy off, with
two of my old teddybears, Eugene and Gregor, tucked in
with her. I sat with my feet up on the railing and read Virginia
Woolf.

It would be on a day like this that our father would
arrive. He'd just come to the top of the stairs and . . .

I couldn't imagine what we'd say to each other. My
imagination failed me. Hetty kicked her legs, bouncing
Gregor around with her feet (he was a tall, athletic, rather
Germanic bear, and looked as if he enjoyed it). Squinting into
the sunlight, I thought about how enjoyable the warmth of
the spring sun was, and how beautiful my perfect feet, before
immersing myself in the book again. I read: 'The truth is,
I often like women. I like their unconventionality. I like their
completeness. I like their anonymity.'

When I looked up, I saw a cheerful *Hi there!* emblazoned
on the front of a yellow T-shirt. I put down my book and

stood up. 'Hi there, Alex,' I said, sardonically. Like me, he often wore clothes that he got for next to nothing at an op-shop. Why else would he wear a T-shirt with that on it?

'Hi,' he said, looking suddenly shy.

'Well, hello!'

'Greetings!'

'Salutations, even. How did you find me?' I never had got round to giving him my address.

'I hope you don't mind. I saw the name of this place in a newspaper ad. *Samarkand Guest House*, it said. There can't be too many places named Samarkand in this town.'

'You mean, you really didn't believe that I teleported to northern Afghanistan each night.'

Hetty, as if fed up with this pointless banter, started to complain. I put her nappy back on and picked her up.

'Is this Hetty,' asked Alex, 'who used to be known as Anastasia?'

'Yes. Here, why don't you hold her?' As I handed her over, Hetty threw up, sending a spurt of curdled milk in a parabola down Alex's shirt. I fetched a nappy and attempted to wipe it away, but a yoghurt-like blotch remained.

Sophie came back from her shower, thick hair dripping water. 'Hetty just threw up on Alex,' I told her, 'and I can't get it out.'

'You'll have to take off your shirt so it can be washed out,' Sophie said to him. 'It'll dry in a minute in this weather.'

I was dispatched to the laundry to wash out the spot by hand. I bent my head to the task, a teenage Lady Macbeth ('Out, damned spot!'), aware of Alex out on the verandah with Sophie, without his shirt on.

When I got back they had obviously introduced themselves and were deep in conversation, Sophie lying in the hammock with Hetty latched to her breast and Alex leaning against the railing talking and waving one arm about in the air. He had a smooth, hairless brown chest and neat nipples.

Feeling like a servant, I pegged his shirt onto the line. Alex and Sophie continued to rave on to each other, and when the shirt was dry I took it off the line and surreptitiously sniffed at the place where the sick had been. It still smelt slightly of regurgitated milk and, deliciously, ever so faintly of Alex.

I took him around to my room, where he stood and looked about before choosing a collapsing wicker chair in a corner.

'I like your sister,' he said. 'You're lucky. I always wanted a brother or a sister.'

'Yes, sisters can be good to have. Annoying, too, sometimes.'

'There's just one thing, Persephone. Do you mind if I call you Kate?'

'Oh. Okay. Why?'

'Because it's your name,' he said. 'Though I like the idea of Persephone – didn't she live half her life in the underworld and half on earth? When she's here she brings the spring, doesn't she?'

I said, 'I'll get us something to eat. Have you had lunch?'

I left him to look after Hetty and ran downstairs and constructed several thick roast lamb and tomato sandwiches. 'What a lot of food,' he said, when I came back with it.

Being taken by surprise had made me astonishingly hungry, but I tried to eat slowly. Alex chewed thoughtfully, and shook his head politely when I offered him the last sandwich on the plate.

'So your mother died and you have no brothers and sisters. It must have been lonely for you.'

'It was. Just me and my father. We used to see a lot of his parents, but he was an only child too, so there were no cousins or anything. I used to love coming up here to see my other grandparents! But then when my mother died, I only did a couple of trips by myself on the plane to see them before they died as well.

'Until I decided to come back for a while, and revisit the old place.'

He wiped his fingers with a handkerchief which he took from a pocket of his trousers, stood up, and went to scrutinise the pictures I had papered all over my walls. They were a record of everything I had ever liked or taken a fancy to. There was a sheep standing at the top of a chute with an uncertain expression on its face, a line of galahs on an outback fence, a child from the Amazon strapped to its mother's back, and hundreds of others.

'How long have you been collecting these?' he asked.

'Years. Almost my whole life.'

'Yes . . . I can see that.' He knelt down on the floor and looked searchingly at examples of my early period – wonky-edged pictures of fluffy kittens and puppies cut from women's magazines, along with a few well-chosen examples of chocolate cakes and icecream sundaes.

'I used a stepladder for the later ones.'

'Uh huh!'

When he lay down on the bed again, it seemed a perfectly natural movement. He was so close I could smell the sweet odour of his skin. He put his hand out to Hetty and she grasped his finger. He wore a bracelet around one wrist, a perfectly plain gold band.

'So – do your parents run this place?'

'No. Lil does.'

'Would that be the old lady I met on my way up the stairs, who told me where you'd be? She seemed to know who I meant when I asked for Persephone.'

'Yes, that was Lil. We don't have parents.'

Alex looked up at me.

'They're – not here. We just live here with Lil. She's not related to us or anything.' It sounded so feeble that I wanted to add, childishly, that Sophie and I were just there for a little while. Just till our father got himself sorted out and came back for us. The story that I'd been telling myself my whole life.

Hetty started to wail. She often started up like that, without any whimpering preamble. Hunger for her was not a gradual thing, but a sudden and urgent necessity. I picked her up, and Alex stood up to go, and the moment when I might have told him things had passed.

The Red Notebook

Music: Crowded House, 'Weather With You'

Spring has hardly begun, but suddenly it's like summer.
It's so hot, the sky cloudless, the grass crackling under our
feet, bindis spiking our toes. We all sleep fitfully, sheets
flung back, our dreams interrupted by mosquitoes. Mozzie
nets are brought out, aired on the verandah in the warm,
gusty winds, and strung up above beds. We run cool water
over our wrists from the tap, douse our heads, and stand in
front of the fan. Windows and doors are left wide open,
always. Our house is like a tent in the desert. The night is
furred and dark.

The Yellow Notebook

The girl with the yellow hair goes again to the cafe, hoping
to meet the boy she met there before.

But he isn't there.

Disappointment is like ashes in her throat.

After that, Alex visited Samarkand often, and it appeared that he was coming round to visit Sophie as much as me. He and Sophie played Monopoly on the verandah while I bent over my books, and their voices floated across to me and made me irritable and anxious that I was missing out on something. Alex turned out to be a Monopoly hog. He bought up whole rows of houses, rented them out for a fortune, accumulated money like a miser. 'I'm not playing that game with you any longer,' Sophie declared, scooping up the board and tumbling everything into the box with a flick of her hair.

So they played noughts and crosses in a shaded corner of the verandah instead, and cards (Snap, mostly, their hands shooting out like blades), while Hetty lay naked on a bunny rug. I listened to Sophie's shrieks of laughter. She hadn't laughed like that in a long time. She became pink with pleasure. She ran barefoot to the kitchen for lemon drinks, and spilt them off the tray on the way back.

Sophie cut Alex's hair, sitting him on a chair on the

verandah, a towel round his neck, a bowl of water and a comb on the verandah rail. She snipped carefully at his dark hair, brushing loose strands away from the nape of his neck with her fingers. I prowled past with a book in my hand, feeling like an outsider. Alex's neck was so smooth, I wanted to reach out and caress it.

One day, after I'd done enough study for the time being, I went down to the park. Sophie and Alex were each sitting on a swing, chatting, drifting idly to and fro with Hetty on Alex's lap. They looked up at me when I arrived as if they'd forgotten who I was.

The exams were only weeks away, then days. Friends from school rang in a panic – they had not, they swore, done nearly enough work. This was obviously an exaggeration, but I told them not to stress. I was laid-back Kate who always pretended I did absolutely no work at all.

Only Marjorie appeared unworried, but her calmness hid a deep panic. She always made cakes when she needed to unwind, and now she began a baking frenzy. She stood in her kitchen with a spotless apron over her dress, sifting soft white flour from a great height into a bowl. She creamed butter and sugar, beat eggs and added them one at a time, spooned batter gently into greased cake tins, and dropped spoonfuls of mixture onto trays, in a ceaseless, tireless rhythm. She made plain sponges, chocolate sponges, butter cakes, butterfly cakes, tea cakes, fruit cakes, ginger cakes, cup cakes, Anzac biscuits, shortbread, melting moments, florentines and scones – many of these on the same day.

'How about making an orange poppyseed cake, or blueberry muffins?' I asked her, but she looked blank. If it wasn't in *The Australian Women's Weekly Cookbook*, 1970 edition, it wasn't part of her universe.

'How's your Russian prince?' she asked.

'He's okay.' I had still not introduced Marjorie and Alex to each other, or told her that he wasn't a Russian prince, just a boy with an interest in politics who lived in an old garage and stacked supermarket shelves at night.

'Bring him round for tea.'

So I did. I felt rather nervous about suddenly placing together two important people in my life, in case some previously unknown chemical reaction might take place. As Alex sat down at the table I watched out for fizzings, foamings or explosions, but there were none. They watched each other shyly, and said very little. But there wasn't much need for talk anyway, there was too much food to be admired and eaten. Teaspoons tinkled against bone china; Marjorie got up to refill the teapot.

Alex ate sparingly and, despite my best efforts, there was still plenty left over. Marjorie urged us to take the rest with us. I took some home to Sophie, and Alex dropped the rest in to the people at Hope Springs.

The next time I invited Alex to tea at Marjorie's, he declined.

'Why? Don't you like Marjorie?'

'No. That's not it,' he said, and looked uncomfortable. 'Marjorie is fine – she's lovely.'

Then he said, 'It's because there's too much. Too much food. Too many urgings to eat. I hate that. It reminds me of my grandparents.'

But I saw Alex and Marjorie together in the park one day. They were sitting cross-legged, face to face, ripping leaves apart as they talked, their fingers working avidly. Marjorie's bicycle lay sprawled beside her on the grass, and she still wore her helmet, crammed on top of the straw hat she always wore when she went out. The day was stinking hot, and her cotton dress was limp; even Marjorie couldn't always look immaculate in this heat. But she was so absorbed in her conversation with Alex that there was a kind of luminosity about her. Neither of them noticed me at all, and I walked on, feeling lost.

Alex came to the cafe one Saturday afternoon, where he sat for hours with a strong black coffee, poring over the newspapers with his forehead creased and his fingers playing around his mouth and chin. People kept coming up to him – the thin boy who sold the socialist newspapers, a bouncy girl in overalls with dark curls and the face of an Italian madonna, an older man with grey hair in Volley sandshoes with the backs cut out of them. Alex greeted them with a delighted smile and gestured for them to sit down. At one stage there were six people at Alex's table, all talking at once, scribbling things on bits of paper and arguing and laughing. Then they drifted off one by one and it was just Alex again.

'Can I get you something, Alex?' called Hannah, heading past with a tray full of drinks.

'Oh yes, thanks,' he said, 'Another coffee?'

'Do you know him?' I asked her. It was the first time I'd seen him in the Dancing Goanna.

'Alex? Oh yeah, he comes in all the time. Everyone knows Alex.'

So when I had thought that Alex was mine alone – my

secret – it turned out that he belonged to everybody. It deflated me.

When Hannah delivered his coffee (with a complimentary biscuit on the side, I noticed!), she stood talking with him for ages, and I thought she looked particularly lovely that day, all rounded breasts and curvy hips and glossy hair. And Alex drank her in (He did! It was plain for anyone to see), and his eyes were all sparkly and his mouth particularly pleased.

How did Hannah do that? Look (and surely feel) so in possession of her own body? How did she inhabit her clothes so that they enhanced her, whatever they happened to be?

Alex left the cafe just before we closed up, waving to both Hannah and me equally. I went home and took the red dress that Hannah had given me, the dress that I could have had adventures in and which I'd hung on the back of my door like a graceful, supple version of myself, and crumpled it into the bottom of my cupboard.

The Red Notebook

Midnight.

Oh Alex. Where are you? Are you packing supermarket shelves with Omo and instant noodles? Are you sitting at your typewriter are you thinking of your mother are you are you?

The Red Notebook

I am sitting in my fig tree and it's the middle of the day and searingly hot. It is also far from secluded – people from offices downtown drive here to sit in their cars or on the bank of the river to eat their lunches, so there are people all around – but in this tree I have always felt invisible, because it is my own world.

Music: 'Hey Joe' by Jimi Hendrix, blaring from a car stereo. I will write this quickly and leave.

Dear Red Notebook, I want no one to ever read you. Because I want to tell you things I would tell no one else.

I always thought that my mother would turn up one day. But now I have to admit to myself that she won't. Well, probably won't, because you can never say never ever, can you?

I keep thinking about how a woman could ever leave her children. I think of her in that red dress, running off for adventures and God knows what. Running away from us, because whatever she wanted to do, we were obviously stopping her from doing it.

I look at Hetty and I love her more than anything in the world. Even though she is so tiny and helpless, she is very strong. I get the feeling that soon nothing will stop her. Her life is all about movement and doing and being!

I don't know how I could ever leave her, and I'm not even her mother.

How *can* I ever leave her?

I'm getting cold feet about going away, and I haven't even told Lil or Sophie yet about my university choices. That I have chosen (chosen!) to go somewhere away from here, away from them. (Whether I get accepted or not is another matter. But I will. Won't I? And if I do, will I have the necessary $$$ to go?)

Now I am talking to myself, Red, instead of to you. But you are me, aren't you? That is the point of you. Talking to you is like talking to myself.

The Red Notebook

Here I am already, scribbling again. No music. Hetty sleeping.

Tonight: dinner.

It is so hot, but Lil insisted on cooking roast lamb. I couldn't eat it. Tomorrow is my first and most important exam, English. Lamb and roast potatoes is impossible. Such a meal would clog up my brain cells. Fish! I needed fish!

So I ripped open a can of sardines and ate them from the tin, standing at the sink. I crunched into the little bones like a cat, chewing and chewing. The sardines made me feel ill – they were oily and warm and nasty – but I had to eat them anyway as Lil was sitting there with an air of wounded pride, working her way through the meal she had spent so long cooking.

I hate myself sometimes for my cruelty and tactlessness. Anyway, now what's done is done.

Sophie (a vegetarian when she wants to be) pushed a couple of roast potatoes round her plate and then said she wanted to go out.

So now I am here looking after Hetty, and Lil is annoyed with Sophie and me for various reasons (me for eating the sardines and Sophie for going out). And I can only say that Tolstoy was right when he said at the beginning of *Anna Karenina* that each family is unhappy in its own way.

I lay on the bed with Hetty and watched as Sophie got ready to go out.

She had borrowed a dress from Carmen, made of stretchy material in shades of purple that drifted across the fabric like high clouds. It was a body-hugging dress that you had to wriggle round on your hips till it sat right. The neckline could either modestly conceal the tops of your breasts or, if you pulled it down a bit, reveal them alluringly. Sophie tried it both ways and decided on the concealed look (to be mysterious is more flirtatious). It had a hemline that made it look like a short dress from the back, and a long dress from the front. Sophie surveyed it from all angles in the mirror, screwing up her eyes and getting a sour expression to her mouth.

Then she took it off and put on one of her own limp dishrag dresses.

I often watched Sophie, hoping to know her better, because she rarely confided in me. Since Hetty was born, we had often lain on her bed together reading. I'd noticed how

Sophie often unconsciously touched her own body, lying on her back with the book held at arm's length above her, running the fingers of her other hand lightly across the bones of her hips and the mound of her stomach. Or she sat cross-legged on the bed, the book in front of her, her neck bowed, pressing the bones of her upper spine and rubbing her back. She touched her face, too, tracing a finger around the shape of her lips, or smoothing the hair away from her forehead. It was as if, while she was reading, lost in another world, she was also reassuring herself of her own boundaries.

Sophie took off the dishrag and put Carmen's dress on again. 'I've expressed some milk – it's in the fridge labelled breast milk,' she said, approaching the mirror anxiously without her glasses on, fluffing up her already voluminous hair. 'How do I look?'

'Like a tart.' We both loved that word, which was one of Lil's favourites.

'Good,' said Sophie. She put on her glasses. With Carmen's dress, they gave her the air of a librarian who was waiting for someone to ravish her. 'I am, after all, a loose woman,' she said with the hint of a question in her voice.

'A woman with a Past.'

'Exactly.'

Sophie crammed her feet into a pair of high-heeled sandals and stood poised, as if for flight. She had such an air of heightened expectation that it made me breathless. I had offered to look after Hetty so Sophie could go out, but now I wanted to tie my sister down; take her hand and sit her on the bed and order her, 'Stay.' I had the feeling that Sophie was a woman who was about to Do Something. It was that dress, her air of distraction, the faint odour of guilty delight that she had somehow acquired as she dressed.

Sophie pecked Hetty on the cheek and was halfway out the door when she turned around with a stricken expression. She took Hetty from my arms and kissed her again, avidly. 'Look after her for me, Kate?' she said, and went quickly.

Her final words disturbed me, with their hint of a plaintive question. And Hetty seemed aware that her mother had left the house, and wouldn't settle. I was so sick of her bored grizzles that I ended up spending ages walking around the verandah with her in my arms. The noises she made were designed to set teeth on edge, and they succeeded; I tried to soothe her by constant jiggling and soft words of love, but I felt that it was Sophie she wanted.

Oh, Sophie. I wanted her back as well. I kept thinking of the way she had dressed herself earlier, and her critical edginess about her appearance. But why shouldn't I look after Hetty for an evening? Or even for longer? I didn't think of Hetty as entirely Sophie's. Hetty was my responsibility, as well. She had chosen not only Sophie to be her mother, but me to be aunt.

I took stock of Hetty. She was growing and developing steadily. But it was slow, slow, slow. I was impatient for her to crawl and to run and to walk. I couldn't wait till she learned to talk. I longed to discuss Virginia Woolf with her, and see whether she liked the plays of Oscar Wilde as much as Sophie did.

I gave her a bottle of milk, and she slept. But I was incapable of settling down to study. I stood at the window of my room and looked out into the darkness. On the other side of the trees, a laneway ran along the back of the house, and I could hear people strolling through it, talking to each other. 'Come on!' demanded a loud male voice. 'Hurry up!'

At night the town took on a kind of glamour. Lights glittered along roads and through the trees. Mysterious shadows lurked in the dense vegetation that surrounded most of the houses. There was something exotic in the warmth of the air and the fragrance of leaves and flowers. I knew that on verandahs everywhere there was the glow of cigarettes and the occasional rattle of conversation. If you walked through the streets you'd catch glimpses of people in houses as transparent as fishtanks, sitting at desks under reading lamps, or dancing by themselves in dimly lit rooms.

Somewhere out there was Sophie, in her tight purple dress.

While I stood admiring the night, Marjorie rang.

'I thought I'd call you to wish you luck,' she said.

'Gee, thanks. I'll need it. What's that noise?'

'I'm whipping some egg whites with sugar till stiff peaks form. For lemon meringue pie. Can I come over? I'm so nervous I think I'll go mad.'

'Of course.'

'I'll have to wait for the pie to cook.'

An hour and a half later, from a deck chair on the front verandah, I heard the sound of a 1965 Holden as it growled its way up the street. Marjorie pulled up on the grassy square in front of Samarkand in her mother's car, and waltzed up the steps with a warm lemon meringue pie in her hands.

We cut ourselves large slices of pie, and I filled two glasses with wine from Lil's cask, and we sat on the sofa outside my room, speaking softly so as not to wake Hetty. 'Well, this is it,' said Marjorie. 'The thing I've been working for my whole life.'

'These exams? You can't have been.'

'Slight exaggeration.' Marjorie took a sip from the wine and sat her uneaten pie on the floor.

I could see her anxiety in the hunch of her shoulders, and the way she stared out at the night without seeing it. A flying fox flapped away through the trees, its strong wing-beat cutting the air. Hetty squawked and then was silent.

Marjorie looked down at her feet, clad in little black shoes like ballet slippers. 'I can't see beyond them,' she said.

'I can,' I told her. 'Beyond these exams is . . . life! The rest of our lives!'

'But we have to get through them first.'

I wanted to tell her, *Stop fretting. You'll do fine in the exams! Before you know it you'll be operating on people's spleens!*

But I didn't. I looked out into the night.

'You didn't tell me Alex was a medical student!' said Marjorie.

A picture came into my mind of the two of them, sitting on the grass the other day, talking.

'He told me he was taking a year off while he thought about what he wanted to do. That was really interesting to me – we talked for ages. You might have told me *that* about him!'

He might have told me that about himself.

Marjorie stood up. She had hardly touched her drink, or her pie. 'Anyway I'd better go and get some sleep. And so had you.'

She looked such a small creature as she walked down the darkened front steps; she heaved the door of the car open and it clunked shut behind her. I watched the red eyes of the tail-lights as the car groaned its way up the road and disappeared, and then went to check on Hetty, who was still sleeping soundly.

I took a sip of the water I kept beside my bed, climbed under the mosquito net and switched off the light. It was well after midnight, and Sophie still wasn't home.

I found that there is a point at which you cease to expect someone's arrival; stop listening for a taxi to pull up or for the sound of footsteps on the stairs. I don't think I slept that night, but I must have. I was only aware of the flapping of moths, the hum of mosquitoes, Hetty's breathing, and my own thoughts.

At 5:30 a.m. Hetty woke, and would not be comforted. Sophie was still not home, and there was no breast milk remaining to feed her. But as I jiggled her on the front verandah in the half-light of morning (bats flying across the sky, back from their evening foraging), hoping not to wake Lil, Sophie returned, coming up the front steps with her shoes in her hands.

She wiggled out of her dress and dropped it on the floor. Sitting down on the bed, she opened her bra and gave Hetty her nipple with a sigh.

And I left them and went to my room and wept.

The English exam went quickly. It seemed that no sooner had we been instructed to turn our papers over than we were being ordered to put down our pens. Three hours passed like ten minutes.

'*So long as you write what you wish to write, that is all that matters,*' Virginia Woolf had urged. '*But to submit to the decrees of the measurers is the most servile of attitudes. To sacrifice a hair of the head of your vision, a shade of its colour, in deference to some Headmaster with a silver pot in his hand or to some professor with a measuring-rod up his sleeve, is the most abject treachery . . .'*

I did what Virginia Woolf had advised. I wrote freely. I did not think of headmasters with silver pots in their hands or professors with measuring-rods up their sleeves. I wrote as if I was neither a man nor a woman (it is fatal, Woolf said, to think of your sex): I was woman-manly. I wrote not only of human beings in relation to each other but in relation to the sky and the trees as well. I thought of things in themselves. I quoted the required texts and drew on my additional reading. I wrote with freedom and courage.

I avoided talking to anyone afterwards because I hated post-mortems, and went home and straight to my room. I didn't care what the hypothetical headmasters or professors thought of my work. I had done brilliantly!

And then, of course, I immediately feared that I had done very badly. And I cared very much what the markers of my work thought of it. I went to the kitchen and consoled myself with ten shredded wheatmeal biscuits with butter, and told Lil, when she asked, that the exam had gone okay.

Sophie and Hetty were out, so I filched my copy of *Anaïs Nin* from where it lay on Sophie's floor and went to the park. I lay down on the grass, pulled the book from my bag and gave it a smacking kiss on the cover (the kiss landed on Anaïs Nin's left breast). I found that kissing a book was like hugging a tree. It made me feel better. But because my head was too full, I was unable to read, so I got up to walk through the park.

And there, in the distance, was Sophie. She was lying on

the grass, and Hetty was next to her, lying on a bunny rug. Sophie looked as though she was waiting for someone. She was. A man approached, stopping as he got near them. It was Marcus.

Sophie picked up Hetty and got to her feet. Watching from behind a tree, I saw that she was introducing Hetty to Marcus for the first time. He looked dumbfounded and not too pleased. They sat on the ground together and talked. I pressed myself against the bark of the tree and thought I could smell the sap in the trunk. All I heard from Sophie and Marcus was the odd fragment of word.

Marcus got up again. He took a couple of steps and turned round. He went back to Hetty, and wonderingly, he put out one finger and touched her on the cheek. Then he turned and went, without a backwards glance. Sophie bowed her head and looked away.

Hetty lay staring at the sky. She would never remember him at all. She was too young to even watch her father walk away.

The Red Notebook

I found this sitting on my desk today when I got home.

(a note, pasted in)

Dear Persephone/Kate,
    I came round to see how your exam went – waited a while in your room for you (hope you don't mind). Maybe I'll see you tomorrow.
    Alex

Music: 'All That Useless Beauty,' Elvis Costello (I can't stop thinking about Sophie and Marcus)

The next day, Alex drove up in a car. Already, the heat had made a haze over everything, and my skin felt as if it was smouldering.

'Where did you get that?' Sophie called from the verandah. She wore a piece of cloth tied round her head (to keep the hair off her face), and baby cereal was smeared down the front of her singlet – no bra. She'd lost a lot of the weight she'd put on when she was pregnant, and her cheeks were hollow. Her shoulderblades stood out. I hadn't ever noticed before that her elbows were dimpled. Sophie was all beautiful bones and curves.

'I borrowed the car from Gavin, at the shop.' Alex grinned, and his face was full of happiness and light. 'It even has a baby capsule. I thought we could go to the beach.'

In the car, Sophie sat in the front and put her head out of the window like a dog, her hair streaming behind her. The wind was warm and made my mouth dry. I held one of Hetty's fingers as we sat in the back together; Hetty sucked the fist of her other hand furiously, as if sucking was what she'd been put on earth to do. I watched the back of Alex's head. There were lines of hair running down the back of his neck in whorls like a weather map. *Today will be hot and windy and full of surprises, with possible evening thunderstorms.*

We sat under the trees above the dunes and looked at the sea. A stream of brown water flowed across the rippled sand from a little creek, cutting the beach in two. A flock of gulls stood beside it, as if waiting along a platform for a train. Not far from them, a cormorant sitting in the branch of a casuarina let fall a spurt of shit, which flew gracefully to the ground like a ribbon unfolding.

Sophie sat in an offhand way, her gaze on the horizon. She said, sulkily, 'Rimbaud – you know, the poet – said that a seagull's shit is as worthy of poetry as a flower.' She hit the flats of both hands against the ground in an impatient, edgy rhythm. 'And why *should* poets write about beautiful things? There's so much shit in the world.'

'But that particular shit really was beautiful, the way it moved,' said Alex. 'Rimbaud must have meant ordinary, boring old bird poo, the kind those seagulls over there must be doing all the time, even though we can't see it from here. But look at the moon,' he said, gesturing towards the white disc of it. 'That looks worthy of poetry. The flower kind. The world isn't all shit and ugliness.'

'I bet it stinks,' said Sophie. 'The stinking moon!'

She looked at the sun. 'The coruscating sun!'

'But coruscating is good. It means sending out flashes of light.'

'Not if it's a boiling hot day and making everyone as cranky as hell.'

Alex pulled Sophie to her feet. 'Come down for a swim, then. Kate will look after Hetty, won't you?'

'I love the way the beach stinks,' said Sophie. 'It's all death and decay. Even sand is the ground-up skeletons of dead things.' She pulled her top over her head and stepped out of her shorts, pulling down the bum of the stretchy old swimmers that she always wore in the river. They were brown with river mud and faded from the sun. Alex took off his shirt. He was golden.

'The excruciating sea!' he said, as they walked off.

'Yes! It's full of plastic shit. Supermarket bags. Did you know that they find whales dead with acres of that stuff inside them? How foul is that? Humans. You have to love them. They write poetry about flowers and foul up their own planet.'

Alex dodged a dog turd next to the path, sending up a cloud of flies. 'An exultation of flies!' he said.

I watched as they made their way to the top of the dunes, tossing words at each other. Alex went down, and held out his hand for Sophie to jump down beside him. 'Cowabunga!' she yelled.

They raced down to the waves, and Sophie ran straight in, her arms waving in the air like a caricature of someone running into the surf. They dived through the waves together, and came up with their faces and hair streaming water.

They arrived back smelling of salt, and plopped down next to us. Hetty was lying very happily on a rug, looking at the dappled light beneath the trees, her eyes following the patterns. She'd inherited the same pale skin that Sophie and

I had, and would always have to watch herself in the sun, too.

'Swim?' Alex asked me, but I shook my head.

'Come down for a walk, anyway,' he said.

Cramming on my hat, I took off along the path without waiting for him. At the tideline, I walked with my head down, examining the things that had washed up on the beach. Alex caught me up.

'So,' he said, 'you don't swim?'

'I burn. I get dumped a lot.'

I discovered some little bugs, brightly coloured like jewels, stranded on the sand. Some were on their backs, with kicking legs and bright red bellies. I picked them up, and they started to move around on my hand, and up my arm. They were iridescent, some coloured orange and green, others red and blue. I wondered how they had come here, out of their element, to end up stranded like that.

'What little survivors,' said Alex. We walked up the beach against the wind, and he picked them up too, until our arms were swarming with beetles. I stood in the glare of the sun, with the sound and sight of the sea all around me, the wind in my ears. This was all there was to my life at the moment. The beach enveloped me.

My hat blew off, and I let it. A beetle had reached my shoulder; it flew up onto my hair, and still I was just sea and sand and wind, bright blue and glaring white, and the battering of air at my ears.

'Take them up to the dunes!' called Alex. He had retrieved my hat, and held it between his teeth.

We struggled through the soft sand to where tough, grey beach grass crept over the dunes, and put the beetles one by one onto bits of grey vegetation. Alex popped the hat onto my head, and he left his hand there, resting on top of my hat, looking at me. He bent forward as if he was about to kiss me.

'Don't!' I said, and turned away. 'I hardly know you,' and started walking away up the beach.

Alex ran to catch up. 'Why do you say that?'

'Because I don't. I never knew, for instance, that you were a medical student.'

He laughed, 'Oh Kate.'

'Don't laugh at me. You'd think by this stage I should know the least things about you. I don't. And you don't know me.'

'I know that I like you more than anyone in a long time. I don't need to know *about* you. I know *you*. And anyway, I've seen your diaries.'

This stopped me.

'When?'

'Yesterday, when I waited in your room.'

'And did you read them?'

'A bit. I read a bit of them. I felt guilty, looking, but you'd have to have a will of iron not to read someone's notebooks. Wouldn't *you* look, if an opportunity came your way?'

I looked past him, at all that blue. 'I can't even remember what was in them,' I said. 'I never intended anyone to read them. They were just for me.'

That evening, I stood on the verandah in the dark and watched water spilling over from the overflowing gutters; it was almost like standing behind a waterfall. Sophie had only just now managed to get Hetty to sleep – it hadn't stormed for so long that thunder, lightning and torrential rain must have been a new and startling experience for her. I thought of all the new and startling experiences Hetty had in store for her. Long stretches of life seemed routine and predictable, and then there were the startling bits.

When the storm finished, I went across the road to my fig tree without telling anyone where I was going. I embraced its damp trunk and then hoisted myself up into the dark branches with my notebook between my teeth.

The Red Notebook

Writing in the dark again. It makes me feel free, not being able to see what I'm writing. And, as usual, I am invisible in this tree. My magic cloak.

The truth is today I wanted Alex to kiss me or put his arms around me or something, yet I didn't want him to, as well. I don't want to get involved with someone in the middle of my exams and when I'm planning to go away. If anything happens, I want it to last.

I think about Anaïs Nin relishing her life so much, all the pain and joy. She embraced everything. The world was a continual surprise and delight to her. She considered her life's work to be her life itself, and the recording of it in her journals. Hardly anyone understood her novels, because they were about what goes on inside people's heads. But why should novels be about the big, important things – war and politics and so forth? Why not about the psychology of people, and the way they see the world?

She lived till she was seventy-four – about the same age as Lil is now. The only picture I have of her is the one on the cover, where she is exquisitely young and beautiful. What sort of old woman was she? I bet she kept living her life to the full, and wearing beautiful clothes and putting on make-up, and having lovers, and thinking and writing and feeling and loving her life. Feeling the sun on her skin.

I long to be as brave as she was. When you think of it, living your life *is* what you were put on earth to do. And to do it well.

My options are: stay here, sitting in my tree, being invisible when it suits me, or put on that red dress that Hannah gave me and grow into it.

The Yellow Notebook

Finally, after going to the cafe again and again (she ate an incredible number of plates of seafood spaghetti, though not all at once), the girl with the blonde hair (Katerina) saw the beautiful young man again. Alexander.

He was sitting at a table in the corner, and the candlelight made his skin seem golden. His face was all in shadow; she couldn't tell whether he was looking in her direction or not.

But he did see her, because he stood up, and smiled, and came to her table. They talked for hours, about poetry this time, and more than anything she wanted to be bold enough to ask him to come home with her.

After that, I often found myself, in between exams, at the door of Alex's garage. I didn't ever mean to visit. Each time I turned up I thought, *So. Here I am again.*

We cooked meals together, on the two gas rings of the little camping stove in his room. Pasta or noodles and stir-fry. Pancakes, once, which I burnt and then fed to a scavenging magpie in the garden. We ate outside Alex's back door in the twilight, sitting at a wobbly outdoor table near the water tank. Vivienne, the old woman who owned the house at the front, sometimes waved to us, or brought us biscuits and lemonade.

I learned about Alex's family. He was the only child of another only child of Polish refugees after the Second World War. His grandparents had had other children, from their first marriages, but everyone in each of their families had died in the war, except for a few distant relatives who were still in Poland. They met on the boat coming out, and Alex's father – their son – represented their hope for a new life.

Perhaps that was the reason for Alex's lean intensity.

There was so much ancestry distilled in him, such a concentration of history and hope, it seemed too much for one person to bear.

The stories from his childhood enchanted me.

I imagined him when he was young, a solitary little boy playing under the table while the grown-ups talked, aware of the tinkle of teaspoons above his head. 'My grandparents were happiest when their friends from Poland visited. The food – you can't imagine the food. And the cakes . . . They often spoke in the language they had grown up with – I think they got carried away and forgot which language they were using. There was a lot of laughter. And sometimes a silence came over the room, and there were sighs, and a few tears. They never spoke about what had happened to them during the war except among themselves. Sometimes they hinted at things. "*With nothing we survived*," they said. And their other mantra: "*Australia has been good to us.*"'

Alex was infused with his grandparents' melancholy. At those times I just liked him so much, with his whiff of the exotic, his threads of connection to somewhere else.

Once, Alex said something for which I could find no reply. 'My grandfather told me very little about the war. It was too much, you see. Too much pain in remembering. He did tell me once how they were rounded up into ghettos. Kept from their work, crowded into inadequate buildings, many families together, awful conditions.'

He looked at me.

'And then lorries came in the night and took them away.'

There was the other side to him, the boy who used to come to Lismore to see his mother's parents. They fed him on roast lamb and scones, and took him to the municipal pool to swim, and helped him build a billycart to swoop down the street in.

I don't know whose idea it was to reorganise the shelves at Hope Springs, instituting a new category called Men's Literature and renaming the shelf previously reserved for women's books as just Literature. It was one of those ideas that simply happened, born out of our elation and shared silliness.

Men's Literature turned out to be an enormous section. Whichever way you looked at it, men had certainly had a good go at writing novels over the years.

I found a wonderful copy of *Great Expectations*, with an old embossed cover and thick paper that was spotted with brown marks. *Peggy to Betty, April 22, 1898*, was the inscription inside. Because of its antiquity, it had a premium price on it – a whole $10. I had a perfectly good copy of my own, so I didn't need it, but before I shelved it under D in Men's Literature, I scribbled a note and put it inside the cover:

Dear Reader,

I think this book is wonderful. If you haven't read it yet, please buy this copy. You must admit it's lovely-looking, and very old and all that, but most importantly, it has some beautiful writing in it.

Hope you enjoy it!
Another Reader

A man was leaning against the shelves nearby, reading a book called *Women in Love*. More Men's Literature. He had a day's growth of orange stubble on his face, and wore a navy singlet. The shop was very hot; the only ventilation was from a large gap at the front where a roller door was raised during the day. It was too hot to be reading literature of any sort. Anyway, what would a man know about women and love? Quite a lot, evidently. They seemed always to be writing about it.

'What do you know about love?' I asked Alex, after the man had left without buying the book and having replaced it in the wrong section entirely. I retrieved it and took it back to where it belonged, among the men.

'Not a lot, really,' said Alex, echoing my flippant tone. 'You?'

'Only what I've read in books.'

'Oh Kate. That's sad. That's really sad.' His remark was halfway between seriousness and banter.

We sat on the sill of the roller-door gap, trying to pick up any whisper of breeze that might make its way down the alleyway. No one else came in. It was too hot to be hanging round in stuffy bookshops.

A parrot screeched from the yard of the petshop that backed onto the laneway.

'I hate that,' said Alex. 'Birds in cages. I keep wanting to liberate it.'

'You must have a love story,' I said to him. 'You're so old and you've been to university and everything.'

'I'm not that old.'

'As old as Sophie. She has a love story.'

'Marcus?'

'She told you?'

'Of course.'

'If you tell me your love story, I'll tell you mine,' I said.

Alex looked at me with surmise. 'All right.'

He pushed his hair out of his eyes and stretched out his legs. Alex was so angular when he sat; his elbows and knees were like a geometry lesson.

'You know how I told you that when I was nine, my mother died? I had no brothers or sisters – it was just me and my father. He worked an awful lot; he's an industrial chemist. And in most of the school holidays he had no time off. Anyway, when I was ten I decided I didn't want to go and spend the days with my grandparents – his parents – during the holidays as I had the year before. They were overprotective and clingy. They fed me too much.

'My father said I could stay home as long as I went to the holiday care centre that was running in our suburb. So I went to that every day – it wasn't far to walk. It was held at the local oval, and we mostly played sports and games, which I didn't much like. In wet weather we played board games under the grandstand. There was this beautiful girl running it. Her name was Maria. I think she was a uni student on a holiday job. She seemed pretty inexperienced with kids, and got flustered easily, but she was nice.

'I was in love with her. People think kids of that age don't fall in love, but they do. I adored her. I'd get up every day with anticipation. I was longing to see her again. I loved the way she smiled at me, and her laugh, and the sexy dresses she wore – you could see her cleavage when she leaned over. I wasn't the only boy who looked.'

'I used to follow her around, help her carry stuff. I think she was finding the job quite difficult. There were a lot of kids, and it was frantic and noisy.

'One day I got there extra early, and I was the first one there when she arrived. I ran across the oval towards her, calling out hello. I ran up to her and took her hand. And there was this – this *split second* where she recoiled from me. I felt a kind of distaste and fear coming from her. It was just an instant, just a feeling.

'I stayed at home for the few remaining days of the holidays. I pretended to my father that I'd gone out, but I came back to the house and spent my days watching TV and reading comics.'

Alex looked across at me.

'I learned then that you can be too needy. You can overwhelm people.

'There've been other girls, of course, at high school and university. But when you asked me about love, it was Maria I thought of. Funny, isn't it?'

The parrot screeched again. 'Now it's your turn,' he said.

'Another day,' I said, hopping down from the sill and going inside to where the work of shelving the rest of the Men's Literature awaited me.

One day we lay on my bed, one at each end, while I went over my notes for the next exam. My hand sneaked out often to Anaïs Nin, or Virginia Woolf: I stole snatches of their writing to entertain myself.

Alex reclined with the newspaper – a Sydney broadsheet. It flapped like a giant bird as he turned the pages. Alex was also bird-like – an intelligent crane, perhaps, his head on one side, thoughtful, absorbed. He looked as though he ought to be sitting in a cafe. (In fact, he often did sit in a cafe: the Dancing Goanna. When I turned up to work on Saturdays I could have sworn that some of the molecules of his breath still drifted through the rooms.)

I ran down to the kitchen and constructed towers of biscuits and cheese, bringing the plate back to my room and placing it in the middle of the bed where we could both reach it. I crammed each morsel of food into my mouth with frank hunger, demolishing most of the plateful by myself before Alex could so much as reach a languid hand out from behind his newspaper.

We never touched, but I could feel how the depression Alex made on my bed made me tilt slightly towards its centre. I looked at him as he ate. He stopped reading while he was chewing and gazed thoughtfully out of the window. Late afternoon sunlight streamed in, revealing the flaking paint on the walls. Then Alex looked over at me and smiled. He simply smiled, and then returned to his newspaper. I went back to my books.

And always, between reading, we talked. I told him about growing up in this house with Lil and Sophie. If I told him nothing about my parents, and my life before Samarkand, it was because I didn't remember. It was as if I was reborn here, in this house.

I felt that I had at last found someone I could be myself with. I didn't feel that I was a girl when I was with Alex, or that he was a boy. I felt that neither of us belonged anywhere except with each other. He was on my side.

Despite this, there was one thing that I concealed from Alex. I didn't tell him of the night I played with my father in the swimming pool of the motel, or my hope that my father would come back one day and claim me.

The Yellow Notebook:

She sees him at the cafe, often. He smiles at her from
behind his newspaper, and then takes his coffee and strolls
over to where she is sitting. The scrape of his chair makes
the floorboards shudder as he sits down. His hand brushes
her sleeve as he reaches across the table for the sugar. He is
so beautiful, and he has become so familiar to her that
sometimes she thinks she has stopped breathing. They talk,
of trivial things sometimes, and sometimes of books. But all
the while, underneath the talk, there is another current
running. It is as though they know each other's essence.

One night she says, casually, 'Come back to my place.'
He accepts, and they pull on their coats and scarves, and
walk together through the frosty streets, never touching.

In her room, he wanders around and looks at
everything while she puts a match to the kindling in her
fireplace and pours some absinth into two glasses. But as
they sit down on the sofa, a movement in the garden
catches her eye. She sees something glitter.

It is her fox. She goes to the door and opens it, and

the fox pauses, wary, but does not run away. She had forgotten to fill its bowl with milk, so she fetches some. The fox waits for her to pour it out. Then she retreats, and watches. It waits till it considers she is at an acceptable distance, and then comes forward to drink.

The boy is crouching beside her. 'You're taming it,' he says softly.

This is the first time she's thought of it this way. 'Yes,' she answers, I suppose I am.'

'And he is taming you. Soon you will be unique in all the world to each other. Then you will need each other.'

'We've read the same books,' she says.

'Yes,' he says. 'We have.'

The Red Notebook

Today I heard the sound of a typewriter as I approached Alex's garage. The garden was quiet, and the sound continued, little rushes at a time. Electric typewriters don't clatter, they make a swift *whoosh-whoosh-whoosh* sound, almost as though someone is throwing darts at a dartboard.

I wondered whether I should interrupt. I couldn't imagine what writing a novel would be like. Once you got a flow going, would it hurt to be halted mid-stream? Perhaps the Muse (whoever she was) was perched even now on the edge of his typewriter (I imagine muses to be weightless, so she wouldn't tip it over). Perhaps all nine Muses were gathered there together in a superhuman show of support.

The typing stopped.

I peeked in the door, and Alex must have sensed that someone was there, because at the same time he looked sideways, and we caught each other's eyes. (Caught how? tangled up in a net? Or with a hook? Or caught like hands reaching out to each other? No, a hook, something vicious.)

He smiled. I took his smile as permission to enter. Screwed-up pieces of paper littered the table next to him.

As usual, he made coffee, and we had it black and sweet, with stale walnut bread. I glanced covertly at the typewriter (I have always wanted to glance covertly, and it is harder than you imagine, to glance secretly at something in a room where there is very little else to look at).

'I'm not writing my novel,' said Alex, noticing my not-so-secret glance. 'I'm writing a letter to my father.'

It was the day I found him at his typewriter, writing a letter to his father, that he told me he'd decided to go away. Afterwards, I couldn't remember his exact words, but they were something like: 'I can't live in Vivienne's garage for the rest of my life.'

He got up from the typewriter and made two cups of strong coffee. He held a cup in each hand, and while he talked he moved his hands about, so that liquid splashed over the tops onto the floor. 'I've thought about what I want to do. I know now I'm never going to write that novel. I've applied to go back into Medicine next year. Before – when I dropped out – I felt that I'd just rushed into university after school. You know, you do your final exams, and then you get your marks, and you do a uni course – without ever thinking about who you are or where your life is taking you. I think some people spend their whole lives like that – just doing what is expected of them. Being busy all the time. No time to think, or reflect. No time to hang about doing nothing much.' He finished, looked down with surprise at the cups he held in his hands. He gave me one.

I couldn't take it in. Even though Alex's living situation looked temporary and makeshift in the extreme, this all seemed very sudden. He looked at me with a mixture of embarrassment and pleading. 'You'll be going away soon yourself, won't you?'

'Maybe.' I was feeling less and less sure about this. It depended on how I did in the exams, and whether I got into the course I wanted, and money, and getting up the courage to tell Lil – too many variables to be sure. I took a sip of coffee, and it was strong and bitter.

'But you're not going straight away?'

'No, not straight away.'

'After my exams finish?'

'Sometime soon after that.'

'Don't look like that,' he pleaded. 'We'll always know each other. We're friends, aren't we? It's not the last you'll see of me, you know that.'

And before I left he handed me a book he had sitting on his table: *Good Blonde & Others*, by Jack Kerouac.

Soon after this, I saw him with Hannah in the street, Hannah eating an enormous icecream, which she handed to him for a lick. As he took it, Hannah bumped into him accidentally-on-purpose with her hip, and he smilingly took a bite of the icecream and then bumped her back, and I crossed to the other side of the street before they could see me. I envied Hannah, with her rounded, womanly body, and her easy way with people.

My solution to any problem: Get lost in a book. I went back to Anaïs Nin, and read her account of her mother's death.

I wrote in the Red Notebook:

She said that the pain was deeper than at her father's death. 'I didn't love her well enough.'

She couldn't concede her love for her mother because it would have meant accepting beliefs and attitudes that were a threat to her existence. Her mother wanted her to be someone other than the woman she was. She wanted Anaïs to be the submissive child she once was. So she had to fight her mother's influence. But as soon as her mother died, her rebellion collapsed.

How hard it must be to break away from one's parents. If one had them.

The Red Notebook

Good Blonde & Others, by Jack Kerouac: given to me by
Alex on a day I don't even want to think about; was once
$5 at Hope Springs

I have smelt it to see if has absorbed any of Alex's scent
(which is, exactly ??? I can't describe it). Anyway, I don't
think it has; it just smells of book.

I have put it away till later. It will always remind me that
Alex is going. Soon will be gone.

I stood in a boutique with a strapless piece of magenta taffeta somehow clinging to my torso, while down below a foam of ruffles danced about my ankles. I scowled at myself in the mirror.

I looked vile. My feet (my elegant feet, my radiant feet) poked out the bottom of the dress, and they were the only lovely thing about me. I thought it was very unfair that feet must be encased in shoes on all but the least formal occasions, for they would have been my saving grace.

I was looking for something to wear to the school formal and I could find nothing. I went to shop after shop with increasing despair. In a vintage clothing place I found a pink checked thing with a shirred and beaded bodice that made me look like a birthday cake. In every single dress I tried on I looked like someone other than myself, but exactly who that was I couldn't work out. Actually, at that time, I was at odds with everything.

Alex had booked to go on the bus the morning after the Formal. He hadn't planned it that way, but it had happened, and he didn't want to change it. He said what difference did it make? Alex was all for slipping away without any fuss being made; he didn't even want me to come and see him off. 'My family has always been bad at goodbyes,' he said. 'We hate saying them. My grandparents never got to say goodbye to any of the people they lost in the war. So we never make a big deal about departures. You'd think it'd be the opposite, but it's not.'

The idea of Alex just going without some sort of farewell made me cry inside. I missed him already, and couldn't bear to go and visit him.

'Do you know what?' I told Sophie, when I arrived home from my fruitless shopping expedition, 'I wish I could just wear a suit, like the boys.'

'No girl would wear a suit to a formal,' said Sophie. She sounded so dismissive, so sure she was right.

'I would! Why not? Men always know exactly what to wear for a formal occasion, whereas women . . .'

'Yes, that would be just like you, Kate, to wear a suit.'

'Would it?'

'That was meant as a criticism.'

'But why not?'

'Indeed. If you want to make a spectacle of yourself. But I have any number of dresses here that would do. You wouldn't look exactly glamorous, but at least it would look as if you'd tried.'

Hetty had been feeding voraciously at Sophie's breast, but now she smiled at me with a milky, gummy mouth, and her generosity made me warm to the world and forgive Sophie at once.

Sophie had turned out to be a champion breast-feeder.

'You know, I think. I've found something that I'm really good at,' she had told me. 'After I've weaned Hetty I could be a wet-nurse. I bet there are any number of professional women out there who want to return to work but still want breast-milk for their babies.' While she fed Hetty she leafed through a university admissions book. It was too late to put in an enrolment for next year, but she was thinking of the year after.

'I could do an Arts degree here in Lismore,' she said. 'And then, if I wanted a job, I could do a Dip. Ed. and be an English teacher.' She frowned. 'Not exactly inspiring, is it? But better than spending my entire life as a waitress. What I really want to be is a Buddhist monk. I saw in the paper the other day about an eighty-something woman who had become one. I could shave my head and wear yellow robes.'

'There's that suit in Lil's cupboard,' I said, not able to abandon the idea of it.

'Oh, Kate, please . . . Here, hold Hetty. If I went to uni here we'd be doing much the same classes, probably, except that you'd be a year ahead. You could hand your textbooks on to me.'

'But I'm not going to uni here. Not if I can help it.'

'Oh?'

'I applied for a course in Sydney.'

'Does Lil know this?'

'No, I haven't told her.'

'That will cost a fortune, living down there.'

'I've been saving. And I'll get a job. I can do anything – I'd clean toilets if I had to. I've had enough practice. Here, take Hetty, I'm going to look at that suit.'

I went to Lil's room and found the suit, tucked at the very end of the rail. I had never looked at it properly, but now I drew it from its sheath of black plastic and sniffed it. It smelt very strongly of mothballs, but at the same time it seemed familiar and comforting.

It had belonged to Alan, Lil's dead son, and I regarded it with something like awe. It would be almost blasphemous to wear it, wouldn't it? Lil just about worshipped Alan. I remembered a time when Lil had cried so much I thought she'd never stop. That must have been when Alan died. I'd stood at the doorway of Lil's bedroom, watching her, fearing to go near her. I thought that Lil would drown in tears and take me with her.

I stood with my hands at my sides, and watched, feeling helpless. I knew that Lil was lost to me. I turned and ran to the kitchen, where I sat under the table with the cat. Sophie had tried to haul me out by one arm, but I wouldn't be hauled. I sat with my head curled over my knees, rolled up like a slater.

There were more footsteps. Lil's face appeared, upside down. 'Come on, madam,' she said. 'There's no need to go hiding under there. You're too old for that now.'

She'd held out her arms. 'Come out and give us a cuddle,' she said.

She came in as I stood holding up the suit.

'What are you up to?'

'I look horrible in frocks. I wondered if I could wear this to the formal.'

'I have never heard of anything so . . .' Lil sighed. Exasperated, that's what she was. She often said that I exasperated her.

'Oh, come on, you,' she said. 'Try it on then. If you must. Then you'll see.' She sounded so ominous I wanted to say, 'See what?'

I peeled off my clothes while Lil unearthed a white shirt from the cupboard. I dressed. First the shirt, yellowed a bit with age, then the trousers, light and scratchy on my legs, and the jacket, shrugged on over my shoulders. I looked into the mirror.

I was transformed. I was tall and elegant in that suit, and I looked wonderful. As I approached the full-length mirror my face wore a look of breathless disbelief and appreciation.

'It will never do,' said Lil briskly.

I turned to her questioningly.

'It looks simply dreadful. Dressed like a man!'

'I love it! I love how I look.' I was amazed that Lil couldn't see how stunning I looked.

'People will say I don't know how to look after you properly. It's bad enough that Sophie . . .'

'I'm going to wear it!'

'Not while you're under my roof!'

'Well, before too long I won't *be* under your roof!'

I rushed on heedlessly. 'I'm going to university in Sydney next year, and then I'll be gone and you won't need to worry about what people think of me!'

Lil said nothing for a long time. Then she reached up and removed some imaginary fluff from the front of the suit.

When I had first come to Samarkand, when I was still small enough to fit easily under the table, a terrible thing had happened.

Lil and I had eaten sandwiches, sitting on the verandah sofa together. Lil had put a sandwich on a plate for each of us, and when I finished mine (I don't think I'd ever eaten a sandwich off a plate in my life) I tossed my plate onto the floor.

It made a shattering noise that radiated out until the entire world was exploding with the smash of crockery. I closed my eyes and curled up and put my hands over my ears. I had smashed the world and was waiting for the punishment.

Lil's sadness was harder to bear than her anger would have been. She presented no more objections to my wearing Alan's suit, and aired it on the verandah, then pressed it neatly. On the night of the formal I found that a clean white shirt and a bow tie had been laid out on my bed.

I dressed. My radiant feet were covered by socks and flat black shoes. They would be my secret beauty, and glow down there unappreciated the whole night long.

Lil sat me down to brush my hair. This was something she had always done when I was little, a before-school ritual, to make sure I looked decent. Now she ran the brush through my long hair, and strands came away on the suit, glittering red. Lil plucked them from the fabric and went to the window, and allowed each hair to fly away from her fingers. While she brushed, she talked about Alan, how he had loved words and adventure so much that he went and became a journalist, and was away overseas a lot of the time. Which was what he'd been doing when he was killed, in a bus accident on a narrow road somewhere in Asia.

I felt like a child again, having Lil tugging at my hair

with the brush, and I liked being the focus of her attention for a while. I leaned back and closed my eyes and wondered if Lil ever wished that she had Alan still, instead of me and Sophie. It was strange, the way she'd acquired two girls, and then, not long afterwards, lost her only son, as if some force in the world was intent on evening things up.

As if she had read my thoughts, Lil said, 'Ah well, the Lord giveth and the Lord taketh away.'

She put down the brush and got me to stand up, turning me round and reaching up to fix the collar of my shirt.

'You'll do,' she said softly.

'Marjorie's here!' announced Sophie, coming round the verandah with Hetty in her arms.

For Marjorie, there had been no what-to-wear problem. She already had a rather fetching little dress that I was sure she had packed into her suitcase in a moment of prescience when she'd slipped through time from the 1950s all those years ago. Now she came running up the steps in her shoes like ballet slippers, her short gathered skirt with hot pink and black checks bouncing around her. Her hair was dark as coal, her skin as white as snow, her lips as red as blood; she looked very lively and rather flushed.

I kissed Hetty a hasty goodbye, and then paused in front of Lil. She was the one who moved first. She reached one hand up to my face, and patted it. 'Have a nice evening,' she said.

Marjorie's mother was chauffeuring us in her old Holden. In the back of the car I chewed my nails and peered from the window. 'They might think we're gay,' I worried.

'Rubbish!' said Marjorie.

'Can you go around the block,' I asked Marjorie's mother, 'to give Lil and Sophie time to get there?' They were taking a cab to the venue, so they could watch me arrive. High-school formals were like weddings, or Academy Awards, with people waiting around outside to applaud and take photographs. You had to run the gauntlet.

The Holden pulled up in a line behind several others, and as I got out I could see Lil and Sophie, with Hetty. Milling around outside were all my handsome friends, all dressed up. Cameras were clicking and everyone was squealing and kissing each other. I got squealed at and kissed, and various girls grabbed me by both arms and declared that they *just loved* what I was wearing, and some were being sincere and some were insincere, but I didn't care either way. I was lined up with various combinations of people for pictures to be taken. Then, on the edge of all the onlookers, I saw Alex, tall and brown and slender, in his black beret, and I went up to him.

'Hello, Kate,' he said shyly. 'I just wanted to come and see you on your big night.'

I had forgotten that we were exactly the same height, and could look right into each other's eyes. In the flurry of getting ready for the formal, I had almost forgotten that he would be gone the next morning.

I leaned forward and kissed him on the lips. It was something I didn't even have to think about; I simply did it. Moving towards him and touching my lips to his was entirely natural. Then I walked backwards, away from him, looking at him all the time, for as many steps as I could comfortably manage, not wanting to lose sight of him. Marjorie took my arm and we went into the building.

Marjorie's mother had left the car for us to come home in, and Marjorie and I went on to a party that someone had organised. I wandered around the house and garden, nibbling on a bit of food here, sipping a drink there, chatting to people, laughing, being grabbed from behind, hugged. But my heart wasn't in it. I'd had enough celebration. All I could think of was Alex.

'Do you want to go home?' I asked Marjorie, finding her in the kitchen in front of the punch bowl.

Marjorie turned to me, looking most un-Marjorie-like. 'I don't think I can drive,' she said. 'I've drunk too much. I feel ill. Really ill.' She dashed for the back door.

I spent the next half hour with Marjorie in the back garden while she tried to be sick into a garden bed. But she couldn't be. In between retching she lay on her back on the grass and looked up at the sky and groaned.

'Stop groaning!' I told her crossly. 'It sounds awful.'

'It is awful. I'm so drunk and so sick and I can't vomit, but groaning makes me feel better.'

'Why on earth did you drink so much?'

'Well, the punch was so yummy and fruity and then it made me feel so wonderfully light-headed, and I'm sorry that this is the last time we'll all be together, and I'm worried about my results, so I thought I'd like to forget about it for a while. Kate?'

'What?'

'Don't be snappy with me, Kate. I love you. You know that, don't you?'

Marjorie groaned again.

'Kate?'

'WHAT?'

'Don't yell. I've just discovered something . . . I feel so ill . . .'

'Well, of course you do. Drinking all that punch.'

'No – it's something else. Something really important.'

'What, then?'

'Don't be impatient with me, Kate. I've just now learned . . . that groaning really does make you feel better. When I've got patients who are ill – and they probably will be ill, that's why they'll have come to me – I'm going to say to them, "Groan as much as you like. Go on," I'll tell them, "have a good groan. It will make you feel much better."'

I put one hand on Marjorie's forehead. In the hot night, it felt cool and clammy. 'Wait here,' I told her. 'I'm getting someone to drive you home.'

I got up and ran. I ran through the dark, deserted streets. I ran with the stars and the moon and the slight breeze accompanying me, pulling me along. Growing hot, I shrugged off my jacket and held it in one hand.

I see now that I could have asked one of the other people at the party to drive Marjorie home. Or I could have called Marjorie's parents and asked them to come and get her. There was no logic to what I did. I ran until I came to Alex's place.

He was stirring a pot of paint with a flat stick, and he looked up as I came in.

'It's Marjorie,' I said. 'She's too drunk to drive home. Could you take her?'

Alex replaced the lid on the tin of paint, and scrawled a note to someone, which he left sitting on top of the tin. We walked back to the party without talking much, but all the time I was enormously aware of Alex's presence beside me, and it made me happy.

Marjorie hadn't moved from her spot near the garden bed. She lay staring at the sky. 'The keys,' I said to her. 'I need your car keys.'

'They're in that little bag thingy of mine. Somewhere in the house. You know, people kept wanting to take me home but I said you had it all under control.'

I located her bag thingy on a sofa in the by now almost deserted house. We helped Marjorie to the car and I stayed with her in the back seat, while Alex got into the driver's seat. He sat for a few moments fiddling with the controls of the car. 'It's all right,' he told me, glancing back. 'I'm just finding where everything is. And the gears aren't what I'm used to, but I think I've got it figured out now.'

We set off, and it seemed so ordinary, to be driving home with Alex at the wheel and Marjorie with her head on my shoulder. I directed him to Marjorie's place, and he parked the car in the drive. We got out, and Alex handed me the keys.

I took Marjorie's hand and led her into the house. Lights had been left on in the hallway, and her father called out something from the bedroom as we went down the hall, but I ignored it. I got Marjorie to her room and helped her onto her bed, and put a light rug across her feet. Dropping the keys on the bedside table, I switched off the night-light, and left again.

Outside, Alex was leaning against the front fence with his hands in his pockets. 'Well,' he said, and smiled at me. We set out down the street together.

'Oh,' I said, stopping. 'I've left my jacket somewhere.

I don't know where. Either in the car or back at the party or – somewhere. Oh well, I'll have to find it later.'

We kept walking, and I thrust my hands deep into my pockets, feeling very manly in the suit pants and white shirt and bow tie. I burrowed down so hard that I hit a torn seam and one of my fingers went through into the lining. There was something hard there; I pushed my index finger and thumb through and plucked it out. Under a street light, I stopped and stared at what I had found.

'What is it?' said Alex. "What have you got?'

'It's a stone.'

It was the stone I'd picked up all those years ago, and given to my father, the day after we'd played in the motel pool late at night. I put it into the top pocket of my shirt, and kept walking.

Except it hadn't been my father. The man I remembered had been Alan.

For some reason, this knowledge gave me a new feeling of freedom. I felt light and light-headed. The memory of that stone had weighed me down for years. And it had been there all along, sitting at the bottom of a trouser pocket in Lil's wardrobe. Now I had the absurd feeling that it didn't matter what I did, and I had never felt this way before, so free of anything that tied me to the earth. I might never return to Samarkand. I could, if I wanted to, get on the bus with Alex in the morning and head away from here. Just like that.

There was someone waiting in Alex's garage. It was the thin boy who sold the socialist newspapers in the main street. He'd been sitting at Alex's table reading a paper, and he got up as we came in.

'Sorry,' said Alex. 'I had to go out for a while. Michael, do you know Kate? Kate, this is Michael.'

Michael bobbed his head shyly at me, and said softly, 'Hi.' He had beautiful blue eyes. I'd thought he looked nondescript, but his eyes were his beauty. I thought that perhaps everyone had something beautiful about them, if you bothered to look at them properly.

'Well,' said Alex, 'Are you ready? I'll find an extra brush.' He rummaged on one of the shelves at the back of the garage and found an old brush, stroking its bristles to make sure it wasn't too stiff. 'Graffiti,' he explained. 'I said I'd give Michael a hand.' He held out the brush questioningly to me. 'Do you want to come with us?'

'Yes. Why not?' I took the brush and felt like wielding it at once. Alex picked up the pot of paint (an old pot, left over from painting Vivienne's house, probably), and we set off. For the graffiti, Michael had chosen a wall supporting a railway bridge with a road running beside it. In the daytime it was a busy spot, but tonight it was deserted. The only living creature that observed us was a dog that met up with us near a streetlight, a dog with legs too short for its body, and large tan spots all over it. A car drove past. I wished we had spray cans, something we could conceal under our clothing.

'Right,' said Michael. He seemed sure of himself now. 'FREE THE REFUGEES. Alex, you do the FREE, Kate do THE, and I'll do the last word. Letters so high,' he indicated. We lined up, and began.

I thought of Alex's typewriter and the unused ream of copy paper that he couldn't find the words to fill, the novel that he hoped might help change the world. Perhaps sheets of A4 paper weren't big enough for him. Perhaps he didn't need to write a whole novel. Perhaps three words could say it all, and he needed a whole wall to say it on.

'Car!' hissed Michael, as he saw headlights approach, and we ducked behind the support of the bridge, then emerged again when the car had passed. The spotted dog with short legs had decided that it would stay and observe us, and it sat with a worried and faintly embarrassed expression on its face, glancing at us every so often.

I had never imagined that paint could be so stiff, or brickwork so difficult to paint on. I had rolled up my sleeves, and the paint dripped down my arm and trickled over my wrists. Michael and Alex finished before me, despite having longer words, and as I completed the last part of the E, Alex grabbed my elbow and we departed.

We couldn't stop laughing. The dog gave us a departing glance and trotted off. 'Police informer,' said Michael, and we burst out laughing again.

At Alex's place, we washed the brushes out under the tap outside the back door, and cleaned the paint from our fingers. 'I'd better go,' said Michael. He had been confident and decisive while we were painting the graffiti, but now his shyness had returned. 'Thanks for helping, Kate,' he said.

He turned again to Alex. 'You too. Anyway, have a good trip. Look us up if you ever pass this way again.' They embraced briefly, and he left.

Now Alex's room seemed very small and very quiet. I saw that his few possessions had been packed up into boxes and labelled 'For Lifeline'. The bed sat there, neatly made; it was the only sign that someone still lived there. The suitcase labelled 'Winter Stuff' stood next to the bed, ready to go.

'Well,' said Alex. 'What now?'

'I don't want to go home,' I said. 'I don't want to leave you like this.'

'There's not much of the night left,' said Alex. 'My bus goes at eight this morning.'

'What, then?' I said.

'Let's walk,' said Alex.

So we walked, and the streets were as silent and thoughtful as we were. It seemed natural to head upwards, because Lismore is a hilly place, and by taking the streets that ran uphill we eventually came to the highest point, where a grassy park looked out over the town. We sat down on a seat at the edge of the park, not touching, and I leaned forward, looking down at the place where I'd spent almost the whole of my life.

I sat there with Alex and it seemed that I was poised between where I was from and where I was going. All I possessed at that moment was the present.

'I never told you my love story,' I said.

'No, you never did.'

'I was about two, or three. And we'd gone to a wedding . . . at least, I only have a feeling that it was a wedding.

'I do remember this. We were staying at a motel. It was late, and I couldn't sleep. I was making a lot of noise, talking and giggling. Someone tried to shoosh me – they thought I'd wake up Sophie.

'And then a man picked me up and put on my swimmers, and took me out to the motel pool. Everyone else was asleep. The place was dead quiet. It must have been two or three in the morning.

'We played for ages in the water. I'd jump in, and he'd

catch me. He'd pull me through the water and hold on to me and bounce me up and down. It was wonderful. It really was. I was full of wonder. And all the time there was this sort of quiet laughter between us.

'I don't even remember his face properly. Just this particular way he had of smiling, and the way he . . . *was*. He was quiet and sure of himself. He took a lot of notice of me. Not fussing over me, but noticing how I was feeling. It was just the two of us, and the lights sparkling on the water. Everything shimmered.

'And I can remember the next morning, I gave him something I'd found. It was a stone, from the garden of the motel. I'd found one that I thought was prettier than the rest, and I picked it up and gave it to him. He lifted me up and kissed me on the cheek. He told me that he'd always keep it.'

I took the stone out of my pocket. 'Here it is. He did keep it. Except he died not long afterwards, so I'll never know if he really would have kept it all this time. But I think maybe he would have.'

I looked at Alex, who was regarding me with all of his bright, bird-like attention.

'The man was Alan, Lil's son. This is his suit I'm wearing.'

'How did he die?'

'A road accident. He was overseas. He was a journalist – always travelling. Always adventuring. That's what Lil says about him, anyway. And I really loved him, that night. I don't remember anything else about him – he was just here for a little while, must have come back for a friend's wedding, and he and Lil took us to it. But I loved him. It was special, that time we spent with each other, you know?'

I had spent my whole life fruitlessly waiting for my father to come back. And now it came to me again that I could get on the bus with Alex and go. If I was going anyway, why shouldn't I leave sooner, rather than wait for university to start? And besides, even if I didn't get in, I knew I didn't want to stay here. I could get a job in Sydney.

I didn't say anything to Alex, but the more I thought about it, the more I liked the idea. Why shouldn't I do what I wanted to do? And I did want to go with Alex, didn't I?

I looked across at him, where he sat in contemplation, looking at the lights of the town. He glanced at me and smiled.

I said to him, 'All my life I told myself that the man I remembered that night was my father. I told myself that he would come back for me. But I think I must have known all along that it wasn't him.'

Alex took my hand and held it unemphatically, letting it rest in his.

'My real father wasn't like that. I do remember him – a bit. He neglected us. He used to leave me and Sophie for ages – days on end, it seemed – in a flat with very little to eat. She used to look after me as best she could, and feed me on bits of bread . . . She and I have never talked about this.'

Alex squeezed my hand, and let it go. We leaned forward, putting our elbows on our knees, and watched the light creep over the town.

It was a long time ago that Sophie and I had stood together, barefoot, at the top of the stairs of Samarkand. Even now I could feel every grain of the weathered boards against my soles. My sister and I were not hand in hand; we stood together stoically like little soldiers, arms by our sides, watching our father make his way down the steps. I can see us as though I'm watching myself all that time ago.

We wear faded summer dresses, too small. Mine has gold sunflowers. Sophie is in blue. She has put a red ribbon in her hair.

Our father is going away and I know that he isn't coming back. No one has told me this. No one, apart from him, must know this. Perhaps, at this point, he doesn't even know it himself. I don't cry, because crying would do no good. I can only watch.

He turns around on the lower landing and looks up at us. 'See you, kids,' he says, putting one hand in the air in farewell, his face skinny and sly, his eyes avoiding ours. They are as dry as a parched landscape. 'See you in a coupla days.'

His eyes are the kind of blue that has almost all colour leached from it. Every part of him seeps guilt. He's off up the road, his back eloquent with it.

I know that my father isn't coming back, and I know why. Even at that age (perhaps especially at that age, when children can read people the way dogs read people), I know that he's a weak man. He bears us no ill will, but looking after the two of us is something that is simply beyond him.

That night, Sophie started to talk in her sleep. I couldn't make out what she was saying, but the sound of her voice in the darkness frightened me. I ran to Lil's room, and she woke Sophie, and bundled us into her own bed. We lay in the summer dark, listening to her sing.

Ten little ducks went out one day,
Over the hills and far away.
Mother duck said, quack quack quack quack,
But only nine little ducks came back.

Finally, we all slept. It was the first of many nights we would spend in Lil's bed.

I remembered how Sartre had written that it was quite an undertaking to start loving somebody. That it takes energy, generosity, blindness. He said that there was a moment, right at the start, where you had to jump across an abyss. If you thought about it, you didn't do it.

I had already jumped. I had jumped without thinking the first time Lil had taken us into her bed; I had jumped when I lay near Sophie as a child and listened to her speaking unintelligibly in her sleep. I'd been loving people for years without even realising it. Without thinking, I had leapt across the abyss many times: when I saw Hetty staring at me only moments after she was born, and with Alex . . .

I took up his hand again and stared at his fingers, remembering how Sophie had undressed the new-born Hetty and looked at every single part of her, silently counting her fingers and toes. So Alex's mother might once have examined him.

But I knew now that I would do the sensible thing. I wouldn't go away with him that morning (not that he'd asked me, or even knew what I'd been thinking). I would stay where I belonged, for the moment, with my family.

I asked Alex, 'What are you going to do when you get back to Sydney?'

'Go and see my father. Persuade him that it might be a good idea if we went for a trip to Poland together, to look up the distant relatives over there. My grandparents kept in contact with them, though they never went back to see them.

'Take up my degree again. Write to you. See what happens. Does that sound like enough?'

'That's enough.'

The sun came up, the way it always had, I presumed, though I had never seen it before. Alex and I sat like spectators at a theatre while the light of the world was slowly turned on, illuminating everything. The shapes of trees appeared, and houses, nebulous at first, and then the summer sunlight poured colour through everything, and paled the streetlights to insignificance.

Alex stretched, and looked at his watch. 'Are you hungry?' he asked. 'We could do the unthinkable and go to a fast-food place. And then I have a bus to catch.'

At the garage that he'd made his home, we found my jacket, which I must have thrown down when I fetched him to drive Marjorie home. That seemed such a long time ago. While I put it on, Alex picked up the typewriter, which was all closed up in its carry-case, and put it into my arms, like a baby. 'I know computers are more the thing these days, but some people still use these, and you are very low-tech.'

'What would I want it for?' I asked.

'You might want to write. You've got the secret scribbled notebooks for it. Haven't you read that book I gave you by Jack Kerouac? The piece called "Rules of

Modern Prose" advises, "Secret scribbled notebooks and wild typewritten pages, for your own joy." This could be for the wild typewritten pages. Here – take the paper as well.'

I found myself with a ream of A4 under my arm.

We gave his room a backwards glance from the doorway. Alex carried the suitcase that said 'Winter Stuff', in which I presumed he'd packed the few possessions he wanted to keep, and I took the typewriter. It amazed me that a person could travel so light.

We ate raisin toast and coffee in a room filled with the glare of laminex and vinyl tiles and the clatter of trays. I walked him to the bus depot, and everything seemed ordinary and extraordinary at the same time. A boy with a shaved head sat on a chair outside eating chips. A police car cruised past. A sparrow alighted on the pavement and the boy threw it some crumbs.

We hugged, but I didn't wait for the bus to come. I couldn't bear to stay and watch it pull away through the empty streets, with his smooth hand at the window long after his face was no longer visible.

That first morning, Lil gave us breakfast in bed: strawberry jam on toast, and hot chocolate. I lay there and stretched with the luxury of it. 'Do you know what?' I told Lil happily. 'I love this bed!'

'Do you, darlin'? That's nice.'

'I love this room!' I said, looking around and wriggling my feet. It was the first time I'd ever felt at home anywhere. That sense of peace and belonging and absolute rightness.

'I love this house!'

And later that day, Lil lifted me up and showed me the name of the house, a magical name made of mirrored letters. *Sam-ar-kand*, she said, pointing to the syllables, syllables that dripped off your tongue with a natural poetry.

I felt secure in her arms. I could see my face in that word, but only bits of it at a time. My eyes, my hair, my teeth. I *was* the word. I was Samarkand.

Samarkand.

I got close to the word and whispered it, and my breath

fogged up the glass. Samarkand *was* my breath. It was the first word I ever read.

And that day, when I got home from saying goodbye to Alex, I stood looking at the word SAMARKAND, and suddenly all of my life made sense. I had no need of three notebooks to record my life, I needed only one, because my past, my present and my future were all one continuous stream.

'You're very late home, madam,' said Lil, coming to the door with a tablecloth in her hand.

'I'm sorry, ' I said.

'And what's that you've got there?'

'A typewriter. Alex's typewriter. He bequeathed it to me.'

'Bequeathed it, indeed.' Lil snorted.

'I love you, Lil,' I said, without knowing that I was going to say it. I said it sincerely and helplessly, standing there in Alan's suit with the typewriter in one hand and a ream of copy paper in the other.

Lil stopped, on her way back into the house. 'And I love you too, Katie. Oh, come here, you, and give us a hug. I don't know . . . you come in at all hours – and what's that all over your nails? Paint! And now a typewriter. What am I going to do with you? And what would you do with a typewriter?'

Lil had left a big smudge of vermilion lipstick all over my cheek. I could smell it. I wiped it away with the back of my hand, and said, doubtfully, 'I could write something with it?'

But she had already gone inside to make the breakfasts. 'I could write something!' I yelled out, with more certainty, to her departing back.

The Red Notebook

From Jack Kerouac's 'Rules of Modern Prose': 'Be in love with yr life.'

It was a long time ago, when we came to Samarkand. A whole lifetime away for me, but in the scheme of things, not such a very long time, because I am still only seventeen. If I am lucky enough to become an old woman, like Lil, it will seem just a tiny part of my life. A tiny but important part.

Today, I thought again about the time when I had only just arrived, and in my ignorance, I smashed the plate, the day I thought I had smashed the whole world, and curled up into a ball with my hands over my ears.

I waited for the blow, for I heard Lil get to her feet.

It didn't come. I opened my eyes. Lil was standing in front of me with her arms held out, warding me off.

'Don't move!' she said. 'You might cut yourself.' And she went and got a dustpan and brush, and cleaned it all up. Not another word was said about it.

Today I said to her, 'Lil – do you remember the day I smashed the plate?'

Lil laughed. 'I most certainly do! And I remember later in the day, I was drinking a cup of tea, and I went to put it down on the table and missed. It smashed on the floor. And *you* looked at me with the brightest of eyes. Do you remember what you said to me?'

'No,' I said, not remembering any of this at all.

'You looked at me and said, "Now we're even!"'

Today is January 6, the day of the Epiphany, the celebration of the showing of Christ to the Magi (whatever that was). Of course, no one here knows what that is, so I am still ignorant. We are not Religious and never will be. I got it from the dictionary.

An epiphany is also a revelation of the basic nature of something; a perception of some essential truth, from the Greek, *epiphaneia* – literally, appearance, manifestation, from *epiphanes* – coming to light, appearing.

Now that the results are out, and it is almost certain that I will go away to university, I am getting all nostalgic. I don't want to leave this place! I don't want to leave Lil, or Sophie, or Hetty. I keep walking around and thinking of all the things I will miss. The view – that view from the verandah of my fig tree and the river. How can I move away from that? And the frogs in the toilet bowl. Even the Guests! I will miss it all. (No, not the Guests.) I keep going up to Lil and giving her a cuddle, and putting my head on her shoulder, and she tells me I am a big sook. I heard her on the phone to a friend the the other day saying, 'She's getting that sooky I don't know what to do with her.'

I have just now received the mail. I now get mail! A letter is such a wonderful thing – the smell of the paper, and all those words, written with someone's live hand! I am glad we are low-tech here, because an email wouldn't be quite the same.

I got a letter from Alex, written on the plane to Poland and posted when he got there. He and his father are excited and a bit apprehensive about meeting their relatives at last. He says it will be amazing to meet people who knew his grandparents from *those days*, the days they rarely spoke of, because the memories were too painful for them.

And he says that he hopes to see me in Sydney this year. Maybe we will be going to the same university.

Maybe. Maybe. My marks were good, but I have to see what places I'm offered.

And I got a postcard from Marjorie in Florence. (Italy! The lucky thing.) Lots of tiny writing. I quote her: 'This place is full of paintings, which my parents, of course, adore (and I thought this was meant to be *my* reward for doing so well in the exams) . . . the paintings are are all right, I suppose, as you can see from the pic on the front of this, but Kate – the cakes. *The cakes!* They are exquisite. Magnificent. Unforgettable. I really wanted to send you a postcard of a cake, but there were none. Maybe I'll smuggle some actual cake back for you . . .'

The picture is of a Madonna and child, all gilt and rich colour. The child, held by his mother (yes, *his* – he has a tiny penis) looks out of the picture. He looks, where? To the future? He holds out one arm, reaching out to that future, exactly the way Hetty does. Reaching. Always reaching out.

And the Madonna – she looks at the child. All her attention is concentrated on him. That is her life. To look to the child.

Sophie is looking to her child, but to their future as well. When she does go to university, probably next year, because it is too late to apply for this year, she will be a formidable student. She has already researched the life of Anaïs Nin, and she tells me that she didn't always tell the truth in her diaries. She was not quite the fiercely independent woman she presented herself to be. She had a husband – two husbands! At the same time! – one of whom was incredibly rich, who paid for everything . . .

She has also read somewhere that when Virginia Woolf got married she decided to have books, not babies. If that is so, it seems to me to be a terrible choice. Because why can't you have both? I have to say this, unequivocally. I want both.

Sophie tells me that in the end she chose Hetty, whom she loves above all else. She chose Hetty above grieving for Marcus. The day I saw her in the park with Marcus, the day after she spent the night with him, he didn't want to have anything to do with his baby. And that was when she started on the road back to being herself. To being more than herself, because having a baby has changed her. She says that there is only so much disarray you'll put up with for love. She says that she is no Anna Karenina, and has no intention of doing the modern-day equivalent of walking under a train.

Now that she can sit up, we are reading to Hetty again. When she was a foetus she understood everything – Oscar

Wilde, William Butler Yeats, James Joyce . . . but now that she is a baby she has forgotten it all, and has to start learning everything from scratch. Her current favourite is *The Very Hungry Caterpillar*, which is the best kind of book, having both lots of food and a happy ending. She looks so intently at the pictures, and seems to particularly love the look of the sausages and the cupcakes – and of course, the beautiful butterfly at the end!

When I first brought Alex's typewriter home, I didn't think I would ever write anything with it. I made space for it on my desk, and took it from its case. It was such a compact, innocent creature, like a little hen. I thought that it should get up and start pecking about and exploring its new home, or even racing in blind panic around the room, but it sat there quite calmly.

Then one day I started writing my Wild Typewritten Pages, and I did not see at first how the pieces of my life would fit together. At first, it was like scribbling in the dark, the way I used to scribble at night in the fig tree. It was like going into a dark room with a torch, illuminating everything. There were some things in the room that I expected, and knew were there, and other things appeared out of the darkness and surprised me.

Anaïs Nin said that to write is to descend, to excavate, to go underground, and that is what it was like. I felt like an adventurer, an explorer, descending into my own life and bringing it back into the light.

So now, Red Notebook, it's just you and me again. I don't think I'll ever be able to break the habit of you. You will be the first of many notebooks, each one starting where the last one ended. Anaïs Nin (I don't care what Sophie says about her – I love her writing) said that the present was sacred to her, to be lived, to be passionately absorbed, and to be preserved faithfully in the diary. She also said (will I ever stop finding things she wrote that relate to my own life?) that we cannot always place responsibility outside of ourselves, on parents, nations, society . . . if we accepted a part of this responsibility we would discover our strength.

So here, Red Notebook, is today's offering. This, for what it's worth, is my present:

Music: Crowded House: 'You're not the girl you think you are'

This morning:

I stand naked in front of the mirror and it's as though I'm seeing myself for the first time. I don't care if it's cliched that girls are always looking into mirrors and knowing themselves; I do it anyway. I look like a girl from a nineteenth-century painting, the type of girl who is always gazing wanly at her reflection in pools: pale and slender, with long limbs and hair spreading over her shoulders.

But this is the twenty-first century and it is not for me to loiter palely in the forests like some anaemic nineteenth-century beauty. I have a job to do. I slip into the red dress that Hannah has given me, cram my feet into high-heeled sandals and head to work, like thousands of girls all over the country.

Hands in the washing-up water, calling out orders for coffees, slapping roasted vegetables onto rounds of bread, popping plates onto tables with a smile, I pause for a moment to reflect that the Buddhists or whoever it was were right. *Live in the moment*, didn't they say? I'm too busy to be certain.

The customers are highly amusing. There is a boy with an adorable beard who simultaneously reads Rimbaud and listens to Aretha Franklin through his Walkman; he barely looks up as I slide a succession of short blacks within his grasp.

To people who enquire chattily what I do, I reply airily, 'Oh, I'm making a comparative study of Oscar Wilde and Virginia Woolf,' and they either respond enthusiastically or look completely blank.

A handsome boy is reading an old edition of *Great Expectations*; I ask him if it's any good and he says, 'Oh yes, it's great. I wouldn't normally read a book like this, but I got it at Hope Springs bookshop, in the Men's Literature section. Someone left a note inside recommending it, so I thought I'd give it a try.'

I chat with him for a long time, and both of us smile a lot, and I sway my hips as I depart.

'Flirt!' Hannah hisses.

After work, I scoot through the streets as though I have winged heels. Whisking across roads in front of cars, striding along footpaths, flowing between window-shoppers, and pausing to hover at a fruitstand where I select a perfect nectarine, I move effortlessly through the world as if it is my element.

Voices wash over me:

'But you'd need a bra with that.'
'What's wrong with a bra?'

Two girls meet on the footpath and hug slowly, body to body.

Someone says: 'Lismore is killing me.'

I sleep every second night with Hetty in my room. I love her more than I have ever loved anyone (Sophie, Lil, Alan, Alex. All right – and Marjorie). I fell for Hetty the moment she was born, without even thinking about it. Who was it taught me to love? I think it must have been Lil – she was a sort of Miss Havisham in reverse.

I told Sophie how I remembered being left alone at home when we lived with our father, and the way she looked after me. And the stories she told me – I suddenly remembered Sophie telling me stories! About princesses trapped in castles and handsome princes and frogs and boys that turned into ravens, and sisters helping sisters. 'Where did the stories come from?' I asked her. 'How did you know them?'

'From her,' Sophie replied. 'I got them from her.'

I looked at her, dumbly.

'Our mother.'

It was only then that we were able to talk about her, our eyes unable to meet at first because we share the shame of not having been wanted.

We may never know why she left us. We have to accept what we have, Sophie says, and forgive her, because who knows what caused her to leave us? 'Get on with our lives,' said Sophie, one of the few times I have seen her cry. 'That's what we have to do. That's what we have always done.'

So that is what we are doing, and it's not too bad, this business of getting on with your life. There are all sorts of possibilities for all of us. But for now, I sit after midnight on my bed writing this. Hetty is asleep in her cot beside me. I can hear her breathing and snuffling and turning over. Everyone else in the house is asleep; if you stood outside, my light would be the only one shining out. And as soon as I've finished writing this, I will switch off the light, and snuggle down into the warm dark of my bed, and sleep.

JOANNE HORNIMAN has been a kitchen-hand, waitress, editor, teacher, and part of a screen-printing collective whose posters are in the print collection of the National Gallery in Canberra. She now writes full-time in a shed overlooking Hanging Rock Creek near Lismore in northern New South Wales. Her novels include *Mahalia* and *A Charm of Powerful Trouble*.